Lisa C Hinsley

That Elusive Cure

To Tony,
Have a wonderful Christmas!
All the best,
Lisa

Dec 2014

That Elusive Cure
Copyright ©2014 by Lisa C Hinsley

ISBN-13: 978-1505394597

ISBN-10: 1505394597

Cover design by JD Smith. For more information visit: www.jdsmith-design.co.uk

Editing by John Hudspith. For more information visit: www.johnhudspith.co.uk

The author asserts the moral right under the Copyright, Designs and Patents Act 1988 to be identified as the author of this work.

This is a work of fiction. Names, characters, places and incidents either are the product of the author's imagination or are used fictitiously. Any resemblance to actual persons, living or dead is entirely coincidental.

All Rights reserved. No part of this publication may be reproduced, stored in a retrieval system, or transmitted, in any form or by any means without the prior written consent of the author, nor be otherwise circulated in any form of binding or cover other than that in which it is published and without a similar condition being imposed on the subsequent purchaser.

Also by Lisa C Hinsley

Novels:
Sacrifice
Plague
The Ultimate Choice
Blue Smoke and Madness
Coombe's Wood

Short stories:
A Peculiar Collection

Acknowledgments

Cancer is shit. Everyone knows this but only a select crowd *know* this. As a member of the Cancer Club my experiences have led to this novel, a hope for the future and a desire to find that miracle cure.

That Elusive Cure is dedicated to everyone fighting the good fight or holding the hand of a loved one who is having the battle and everyone in need of a hug: be well.

Special thanks as always go to my husband. He's the rock, the support, the smiles… the everything I could ever need. My deepest wish is to beat the bastard tumors and join him in a long life.

Lisa C Hinsley

That Elusive Cure

Contents

Meeting Janie 11

Phoning Janie 16

Meeting Janie 19

Seeing the Pod 25

Chemo Day 31

First Session 36

Sally Needs Help 43

Dealing with Sally 49

Second Session...57

Cake and Hope 65

Third Session 71

Chemo Day 77

Feeling… normal...83

Out With Janie 90

Cass has News 100

Going to Wales..108

Finding Mr. Newland...117

Mum is Leaving 122

Meeting the Scientist 127

- The Scan 133
- Meeting Sally 138
- Results Day 144
- Bob Gives an Update 154
- Dad and the Machine 159
- Visiting Wendy 166
- Nanoparticle Miracles 171
- Losing It 190
- Dreaming of a Great Escape 197
- Party Planning 201
- Newland Phones 206
- A Plane Crash 211
- An Overdose 215
- An Envelope in the Church 224
- Sally's Getting Worse 228
- Making a Wish 233
- A Belligerent Scientist 239
- Barred 245
- Sally 251
- A New Future 252
- The Headlines 255

ONE

Meeting Janie

"Hi, are you waiting for treatment?"

I looked up from my phone. Speaking to other patients was always better than scrolling through Facebook. "Yup. You?"

She sat down in a nearby seat, a little younger than me, her brown hair short in what I called the 'cancer cut'. "No, I'm finished now."

A green streak of jealously stabbed right in the middle of my chest. Cured. Remission. Words I dreamed of owning. "Just visiting?" I asked.

"Yes." She stared off out the window and over the rooftops that made up the view from the Delamere waiting room. Radioactive signs stuck on the roof of the pharmacy always made me stare as well. "I'm Janie." She turned and smiled, her face warm and welcoming.

"Kathy. Nice to meet you." I shoved my phone in my handbag and smiled back. "Volunteering or just come back to say hello to the staff?"

"Neither, actually, it's you I want to see."

"Me?"

Janie leaned in ever so slightly. "They weren't the ones that fixed me. I was stage four with bowel cancer. Mets in my lungs and my liver. Docs said I was incurable, whatever the hell that means. Slow death, if you ask me. The last scan they did on me before I found the cure showed shadows in the bones of my leg." She patted her right thigh.

I'd heard about so-called cures. Read about them on the internet. Found them in books, newspaper articles and magazines, lured in by those sought after words: remission, cure. Well-meaning people emailed me links to possible treatments and sent me articles about things like fruits that healed, but no testimonials, just a viral video with a sales link, and further research reveals it gives you Parkinson's or some other horrid disorder. Then there were the spices that required you to take a bulk dose, a hundred supplements that might help but who knew. Foods you should eat, foods to avoid, meditation, imagine that bright light and trigger your immune system, and it was all bollocks. I'd tried them all over the last two years, and yet my end date kept creeping closer. Cancer cure myths are big money-spinners. Cancer patients are desperate. The charlatans take advantage, and here was one, sitting next to me, about to tell me to invest in some new miracle.

I leaned away from the woman and crossed my arms. Maybe she really was a cancer patient, still under the thrall of some dodgy scheme. I'd do her the courtesy of listening then fill my arms with my prescribed chemo poison. It was the only real option for me.

"I was waiting here, in this very ward when a man came up to me and said he had been cured. I was skeptical, as I am sure you are." Janie leaned in even further and whispered, "He told me what cured him." She pulled back and looked around to see if anyone was listening in. The waiting room was virtually empty this morning. It was usually full to the point of standing room only. "His name was Dave and he told me how someone had come up to him and told him about the cure. He called himself a 'finder'. Now I'm cured, I get to do the same and 'find' you."

I raised my eyebrows. "So what exactly does that mean?"

"Well, he was chosen as he was sixty-five and just retired. His finder felt bad for newly retired people who get sick. Dave chose me because I looked like his daughter. I picked you because you remind me of my mother when she was young. She had the most beautiful golden hair and the same kind features that you have. I can tell you're a good person, Kathy. And good people shouldn't die young. I lost my mother to early dementia a year before I was diagnosed. She didn't deserve that." Janie looked at the floor. I didn't know what to say.

"I'm sorry to hear about your mother," I eventually said.

Janie looked up. "So, what cancer do you have?"

"Same as you, bowel cancer."

"Oh, I figured you had breast cancer."

I shrugged. Wasn't the first time I'd heard that. I looked young, much younger than my forty-one years and most people assumed I had breast cancer. People my age and fitness just didn't get bowel cancer. Except when they do.

"Kathy Wyatt," Jo, one of the nurses walked into the room calling my name. Young, with a head of blonde spiral curls, she had a wonderful bedside manner. I was happy to be seen to by her. Not that any of the nurses were bad. Considering the circumstances they were all terrific.

"Nice talking to you, maybe we'll run into each other again." I gathered my things and stood. As I did so, Janie pressed a slip of paper into my palm.

"Think it over, but make sure you call me. Please. You won't regret it."

I nodded, still undecided as to what level of crackpot she was. Then I gave her a smile before following Jo into the ward.

Sitting in my comfortable hospital armchair, I pulled the piece of paper out of my handbag and stared at it for what seemed like the millionth time. After I'd met Janie, I'd had a doctor's appointment before the start of the chemo session. Dr. Noble didn't have good news for me. Six new tumors had appeared in my liver and another one in my left lung. The beasties were overrunning me. How much longer could I hold out?

The medicine seemed to take hours to go in, my arm burning as the chemo coursed through my vein. I needed to get a PICC line, but it felt like giving in somehow, having a catheter permanently inserted in my arm. So I hadn't asked for one yet. If it continued to hurt this much I'd have to. For two hours I fought tears at each pump of the IV. Whether it was purely because of the medicine or also because of the bad news, I didn't know. But through the pain, mental and physical, the idea of a cure, the possibility of being free of hospitals, appointments, needles, medicines with cytotoxic warnings, pills, pills and more pills, tests, scans, surgeries, radiotherapies, and the best part of six-hundred days of feeling sick, tired, exhausted and fighting side effects that got worse with each session – well let's just say Janie's words became more and more appealing.

TWO

Phoning Janie

I took the piece of paper from the pin board where I'd put it last week. Janie's number called out to me. What if she did know of a cure – or even something that simply helped? Gave me a few more months on this earth? Jimmy was taking things harder each week as my health deteriorated. Maybe we could take the plunge and get married, before the end came and took me.

I traced my finger over the numbers and then, before I could change my mind, got my mobile and entered the number. I wasn't brave enough to ring and opted for a text message. I wrote and erased five different versions. In the end I decided to keep it short and simple.

We met at Clatterbridge last week. I'd like to know more about the cure you mentioned.

For ten minutes I held the phone in my hand, expecting, waiting for a quick reply. But then the gut-rolling began, one of the side effects from the chemotherapy, and I had to sojourn to the bathroom. I spent the evening checking the screen of my mobile.

I'm not even sure what was on the telly, I wasn't watching. Jimmy asked me what was so important and I told him I'd met someone at Clatterbridge. A survivor. He said the friendship would be good for me. Give me hope. He had no idea.

By the Wednesday lunchtime I'd all but given up on Janie. Then as I threw one of my mother's handy meals in the oven my phone pinged. A message. I almost dropped the dish in my effort to see who it was.

Janie. My heart pounded hard as I touched the screen. *We should meet up for coffee. There's a nice little café down in Thurstaton, near the Wirral Walk. When are you free?*

When was I free? When was I *not* free? I hadn't worked in over a year. Became too difficult between the exhaustion and chemo sickness. The only marks on my calendar were for doctor appointments, and the rest of this week was blank. Sometimes I tried to meet up with friends for lunch on one of the few days where I didn't feel like complete shit. That wouldn't be until next week and I couldn't wait that long. I'd take my anti-sickness pills with me and stay away from anything that was too sweet.

Free for the rest of the week. Could do tomorrow, I think it's going to be dry.

That was also important. Rain drops were cold and burned my skin on contact. Oh, the joy of side effects. Couldn't cope with anything cold: water, metal surfaces, a cool room... Made winter very hard on me. I wouldn't want to walk far trying to hide from the weather.

Tomorrow is good for me. See you at 2.

The reply came quickly and a fluttering of nerves filled my tummy. Stop being stupid, I told myself. She'd have nothing real to offer me, just like every other 'cure' I'd found.

I sat at the table with my chicken pie and dreamed about being *me* again.

THREE

Meeting Janie

I arrived early and sat in my car for ten minutes trying to calm my nerves. I didn't really know why I was in such a state. Jimmy had noticed last night and questioned me during the adverts. I'd been biting my nails, something I only did in the days before scan results or important doctor appointments. I told him how I was meeting Janie today. My stomach felt like it was full of fizzy bubbles, and I told him I was nervous. He told me to stop being silly and go and enjoy myself. Then CSI came back on and we didn't talk about it again.

Now I was here, waiting in the car park for the Wirral Way, watching the dog walkers and cyclists and joggers go by, smelling the fresh air and thinking I was stupid for even pretending to myself that this woman knew of a cure. I should be home, curled up on my bed, the cat at my side, a mug of tea on the bedside cabinet and Jeremy Kyle on the TV to dull my brain. I shouldn't be out, mere meters from the seaside, the trees full of birds and the scent of foxes close, because my stomach was beginning to turn and

I didn't know whether I could keep it under control. I'd taken two anti-sickness pills before I left home. I closed my eyes for a moment and willed them to work.

The dashboard clock ticked over to two PM and I reluctantly got out. I was an idiot, a desperate idiot, hoping for a cure that wouldn't exist. At least I could dream for the next hour. Hear of the madwoman's miracle pill, maybe even buy a pack of whatever-it-is and give it a go, because I literally had nothing to lose. Jimmy said if every supplement I took gave me another one percent chance of getting better I should take it. Enough one percents, and maybe I could tip the balance in my favor and beat the beasts into submission.

"Bollocks," I muttered as I locked the car. Whether I was swearing at myself, the disease, the woman with the false hope or my upset stomach, I wasn't sure. Maybe all of it together. I zipped my coat up, earning a curious look from a walker as the weather was warm today, not that I felt it in the slightest. With my scarf snuggled around my neck and my hands stuffed in my pockets I would have looked more at home in a snowstorm. Eyes to the ground so I couldn't see people staring, I trudged up the road to the café.

"Hi Kathy, I got us a table."

She was at the counter ordering. I joined her in the queue.

"I was about to guess whether you are a tea or coffee person, or do you want something sweeter? They do a luxurious hot choc here. It's a real treat." She smiled at me, and touched my arm for a moment.

"It's good to see you. I'm so glad you decided to talk to me."

My stomach did a flip at the idea of sweet things. "I'll have a tea please." Despite everything, Janie was hard to dislike. She was a pretty lady with open and honest features. Nothing about her said she was going to try and con me. The bubbles in my tummy seemed to expand. Even if all I got was some relief from what was now an almost continuous ache in my liver, well that would be enough for me. I daren't even dream of a cure these days, it just wasn't healthy to get my hopes up like that.

"I won't mess about with any small talk. You want to know what cured me, don't you?"

We'd sat at the table, a big pot of tea between us. Nerves got the better of me, and I sipped at my tea, burning my lips. "Well, I suppose I do…" I laughed, too loud, too forced. A cure. Remission. Normal people just couldn't understand the Holy Grail qualities of these words. "Jimmy, that's my other half, he'll let me buy pretty much any supplement that might work. He's talked about paying for trials the NHS won't fund here if it comes down to it as well, but thank God we haven't had to yet."

"I know what you mean, my other half was the same way. Anything to give us more time together. Gill actually re-mortgaged the house to pay for a course of avastin, that was before the drugs fund was set up. It was nearly £30,000 for a course of that."

"That's insane and so unfair. We shouldn't be put in that kind of a position." I dared to try another sip of tea. "That's what I'm on now. Avastin plus capecitabine. I've had oxaliplatin but they're giving me a break. The doc is afraid the tumors will become resistant."

"That's the combo I was on. Had to deal with all kinds of nerve issues. But you don't want to hear about that. You want to know about the cure."

Here we go, I thought. Give it to me, tell me how much I have to spend for an ounce of false hope.

Janie held her teacup with both hands, and stared at me. "You want to know about the machine."

I couldn't help it. I leaned in towards her, afraid to make a single sound in case I missed what she had to say. A machine? It never even crossed my mind to guess she was going to suggest anything other than a new pill. Raising my eyebrows in expectation I waited while she drank some tea.

"I was told a man called Rich Newland found the machine and hid it in a disused church that he owns." Janie poured more tea into her cup and took a moment to stir in some milk. She smiled at me and continued, "I don't know how true that is, but the fact is, there is a church, there is a machine, and I have the key."

Janie reached into her handbag and took out a large old-fashioned key, a big clunky brass thing that would look more at home in a Harry Potter movie.

"Dave, my finder, he thinks the machine is a gift from aliens." She shook her head and laughed. "But that's a bit too farfetched for me. I can't get past aliens not saying hello, just leaving a machine to be found? No, I don't think so."

"What do you think it is then?" I didn't know whether to believe her or think her insane. At least my curiosity was overriding my nausea, and I was feeling better than I had in weeks.

"It's from the future."

My turn to laugh. "And you think that more likely than aliens?"

"Actually, yes." She sounded vaguely insulted. "Who knows, maybe it's not from the future. Maybe it's one of a few machines owned by very rich and powerful people. It would explain why some of them keep going, no matter how hard they live." Janie shrugged. "Doesn't matter where it came from, it exists and it's in a church in Birkenhead and it *works*."

"What does it look like?" The theory of the rich and famous having developed and kept secret a magic healing machine actually made sense to me. Maybe this Rich Newland was actually a philanthropist, and this was his way of making the technology available to us regular schleps. Which meant maybe there actually was a machine, and maybe it really was possible that I would see this decade out, and maybe many more. A seed of excitement began to grow in me. A cure. Remission. Maybe not so unreachable. I knocked my teacup reaching for it, a barely concealed tremble getting the better of me. "Sorry," I muttered and mopped up the mess with a few paper napkins.

Janie reached across the table and touched my hand. "I understand. I was the same way when Dave started to explain it all to me. It's so much to take in."

As her fingers touched mine tears flooded my eyes, my face hot and prickly as I tried to stop them. "I'm so sorry." I grabbed another napkin and pressed it to my eyes. "I'm not usually like this." Truth was I *hated* being emotional. But this possibility, the slim chance this woman might not be a liar or a crazy person, that this machine might actually exist... Tears welled up for a second time and I struggled to control myself.

"Take your time," she said, her voice soothing. "As soon as you've got it together, I'll take you to it. And to answer your question, it's far better to see it for yourself than for me to try and describe it. But just in case you're dying of curiosity," she flashed me a wry grin as she realized what she'd said, then continued, "it looks a little like a pod."

"A pod?"

"Yes, like out of some science-fiction movie."

I stopped staring at my unfinished tea and glanced at her. Janie was smiling, and I couldn't decide whether her grin was concealing an inside joke. No way was I going to let my hopes get up any more than they already were. This woman that I hardly knew could be setting me up for some cruel trick. I had to remember that. The ache in my liver whispered to me that no matter how silly the idea of this magic machine seemed, I had to give it a chance. Even if I just went to see exactly what this futuristic pod of hers looked like. I rubbed at my tummy as I tried to ease the pain.

Janie pushed the key across the table towards me. "Have you heard enough? Do you want to go there?" I could almost hear the unspoken words, the words hidden between the lines: do you want to be cured?

"Yes," I said and closed my hand around the key.

FOUR

Seeing the Pod

I followed Janie's car, one of those odd-looking little Fiat 500s in lilac, through the countryside and into Birkenhead. She'd said where we were going, and I knew the place. I'd passed by the church on many occasions. I'd even daydreamed about buying it and setting it up as a flat for my daughter, keeping part of the space for me and creating a studio. That was me letting my bohemian side through. The place Cass lived in was grotty, but she refused to move back home, and my dream was to buy her a decent place to live. She had this boyfriend who seemed to be quite handy. I'd let them live there for free in exchange for his manual labor.

We pulled into the tiny car park. I still had the key in my possession, and I thumbed it nervously as Janie got out of her car and walked up to the door. We were in the town center, a stone's throw from the council parking lot I used almost every week. To think this mystery machine had been there the entire time almost made me feel taunted by it. I searched briefly for hidden cameras, my eyes settling on Janie as she stood on the stone steps by the sad-looking church, patiently waiting for me. Taller buildings crowded in on three sides casting the building into shadow.

"You ready for this?" She took the key from me and inserted it into the lock. "You need to give it a little jiggle or the mechanism won't turn." She yanked on the key, her fingers white for a moment as she struggled. Then the key turned. I glanced up at the windows. They were so dirty I couldn't tell if they were stained glass or not. Wire mesh covered each and added to the camouflage. The stone walls might once have been a warm grey, but now traffic dirt covered every surface and the building looked as if it was covered in soot.

My nerves were getting the better of me now, like a ball of static had got inside of me and needed me to jump around to get it out. I stamped my feet and tried to regain control.

"Go on." Janie indicated that I should turn the handle.

"Okay…" We swapped positions and I pushed the door open. It was one of these heavy oak affairs, although the wood was so grimy I couldn't actually tell what kind of wood it was. My belly ached, the tumors making themselves known, and I stepped over the threshold.

Inside was dark, the windows shedding little light. We entered the nave, our footfalls loud on the stone floor. Someone had pushed all the pews up against the walls, piled like firewood and abandoned. A pod-like machine big enough for a single person rested in the cleared space, its metallic hull gleaming like buffed silver. In the background a large cross still hung behind the altar.

"This is it." Janie knelt beside the machine and put her hand on the surface, almost like a lover's touch. "This is what cured me."

Curiosity got the better of me. I could see why she'd said maybe it came from the future, the machine looked like a prop from *Star Trek*. Her fingers danced over an almost hidden control panel. The seal broke and the pod opened.

"This is what you do." She climbed inside and lay down. A type of foam lined the pod, it expanded around her as she got comfortable, cradling her body. "I took four sessions to be fully cured. It's very easy to use and the machine tells you exactly what to do."

"So it speaks English to you?"

"Yes, another reason why I don't think aliens left it. I hardly think they'd program the thing with English. It's home-grown." She pointed to a label above her head. "Besides, it says *MicroHealth* here. I guess they were the manufacturers."

I walked slowly around the pod. The machine was a thing of beauty, the metal flawless, the seams - if there were any – invisible. "How is it powered, it's not exactly plugged in to a socket."

Janie climbed out. "Who knows. Who cares." She shrugged. "Give it a go. I won't close the lid. Settle yourself in the pod and get a feel for it."

I circled it once more, fear growing in my belly. I decided the machine was definitely manmade, I just wasn't sure of *when*. And if the machine wasn't from now, how on earth did it get here? Its very presence made my mind spin with possibilities. Would it cure me? A small part of me was beginning to think maybe the answer to that was a *yes*.

I climbed in carefully, wondering if it would hurt when it worked, like the nettle-stinging sensation some of the drugs gave me. Or worse, like the deep consuming pain I suffered after the first operation. Or like feathers brushing up against my skin, or perhaps I'd feel nothing at all. Maybe it wouldn't even work on me. I'd had bad luck with every other treatment the doctors had thrown at me. Why would this be any different?

A wave of claustrophobia threatened to make me bolt, but somehow I kept control and lay down. The foam mattress expanded around me, reminding me of memory foam, but with a little bit of intelligence. It gave me a sense of security and the feelings of being trapped were simply forgotten.

"Right, I have a list of instructions here." Janie sat cross-legged on the ground beside the pod and showed me a small piece of card. "It's super simple, not sure you even need the instructions, but they made me feel better before my first session." She ran her hand over the smooth shell of the pod, a faraway look on her face. "When you're ready, press your hand onto that pad up there.

I looked where she was pointing. Inside the lid, positioned roughly above my chest, was a square panel that was shiny metal instead of the buffed silver of the rest of the pod.

"Go on, I'll stay here the whole time."

"What, you want me to do this now?"

"I suppose you don't have to. But it's really not a big deal. You should give it a go."

That Elusive Cure

I stared at Janie. "You sure about this?"

"Absolutely. I owe my life to this machine. Trust it." She smiled warmly. "Go on."

I still wasn't ready to be trapped in the pod. "Does it hurt?"

Janie thought about my question for a moment then said, "No... it doesn't hurt as such. More a sensation of warmth. You've had a CT scan? You know the one where you think you've peed yourself and your skin gets really hot? Well it's nothing like that. I felt warmed-up and very relaxed. It's a nice feeling."

"The CT scan...?"

"Yup, but without the peeing sensation. Or the hot skin." She nodded. "It's not scary. Honest."

"But how does the medicine get in?" I sat back up and swung my feet out of the pod.

Janie shrugged. "You know, I haven't a clue. There's no needles..." She frowned as she thought about it. "Maybe it goes into the air and you breathe it in?"

For just a moment I realized I was in an old abandoned church with a woman I hardly knew, trusting her because I thought her smile was honest. I'd climbed in a machine of unknown origin – at least for me. Maybe she was a serial killer, and this was her modus operandi. She'd trap me in this pod, wait until I'd suffocated and then dump my body in the Mersey. Maybe she thought of it like a mercy killing, because let's face it, I was on that road already, she'd simply be shaving off a few months.

The musty smell of the church threatened to overcome me. Beyond my feet the cross that had been left on the wall gave me a small amount of comfort. It seemed to tell me that I wasn't insane for trusting this woman and I should let events take their destined course.

"One last question, how long do I have to be in the pod?"

"That's the best bit. Think of all the treatments you've had, the hours of sitting around as the docs do something else to your body. The pain, the needles, the side effects that last for months… well forget all that. This takes minutes." This time her smile came over as smug. "Lie back down and put your palm on the panel. It's your turn to get better."

"Look, I'm sorry, Janie." I climbed out of the pod. "It's all too much. I'm not sure I can do this. Not right now." Moving away from the machine, I watched it from the corner of my eye as its lid slowly closed.

"Really, you'd rather suffer?" She appeared so surprised.

"You were in my shoes not so long ago. Don't you think all this," I waved a hand at the pod, the church and everything around us, "is odd? I need time to think about it."

"Up to you. It's your life." Janie sounded a bit miffed. I really had to wonder what her motivation was. She was on her feet already and heading out of the church.

I followed slowly, glancing behind me at the pod one last time before Janie locked the door on the surreal scene, a futuristic medical device with a tortured Jesus on the cross hung behind.

FIVE

Chemo Day

Clatterbridge: my least favorite and yet favorite place to be. I missed it when I didn't have sessions. Felt the absence of the security blanket of chemotherapy. But when I was there all I felt was pain and sickness.

It'd been a week since Janie had taken me to the church and shown me that weird pod. She'd been texting me every day since, asking how I was, whether I'd decided to use the machine or not, telling me how it would relieve the symptoms of the chemo, take away the ache in my liver, even get rid of the weak cough that wouldn't go away. Every day I'd thought about the machine, rolling the possibility of being cured around my mind. Despite the utter oddness of the entire situation I really had considered telling her, "Yes," in the days right after the visit to the church. Now, as I sat in the hospital, I was unsure. I hated chemo but it was an evil I knew.

I was hooked into the poison and listening to the people in the bay beside me. A mother was there with her adult son. He was scrolling though info on his phone and telling her in detail what happened if the chemotherapy drugs were spilled. The way he described it, you needed something similar to a HazMat team to clean it up. It would burn the surface off the flooring. It would burn off skin. No wonder the veins in my arm hurt so badly.

The mother shushed him and the silence was worse than the Wikipedia entry he'd been reading.

My phone buzzed.

Hi Kath, hope chemo goes okay today. How are you feeling? xxx

Janie, I'd guessed she'd send me a text at some point today. How did I feel? I was almost finished after nearly two hours of the oxaliplatin chemotherapy being pumped into my vein. I didn't feel sick yet, but I knew that was in the post. The drug gave me major issues with cold things. During the first few days after an infusion even lukewarm liquids were too cold, everything had to be off the boil. I'd be taking a thermos of hot herbal tea to bed tonight so I'd have a drink if I woke in the night. As it was, with the bag of drugs almost empty, swallowing was becoming difficult as even my own spit was too cold to deal with.

Feeling rough. I replied. I felt like I'd been run over by a truck. Every fortnight I came into Clatterbridge smiling and joking. I went out quiet, holding my arm where the infusion had gone in, any good humor long gone. The walk down to the car would be slow.

I hate to press you, but I really need you to decide about using the pod. If you don't feel confident enough to use it that's not a problem. I'll find someone else.

That Elusive Cure

Oh Jesus. I didn't need this. Not today.

The machine attached to my meds started to beep. I just needed a flush of glucose solution to rinse out my veins and I'd be done.

Flush is about to start. Can you leave to come get me now? I fired the text off to Jimmy as the nurse arrived to sort me out.

On my way. Hopefully Jimmy would indeed be on his way. Working from home had seemed such a brilliant idea at first, until having an office in the house became an excuse to work even more.

I needed to reply to Janie, but didn't know what to say. Although I really didn't rate the pod as anything other than a joke, I couldn't help but think about it. It was too smooth, too shiny, too sophisticated… too *perfect* to be a prop. Even the way Janie had found a secret button so the top pivoted open soundlessly was too real. There was something about it that stuck in my brain, like a memory splinter. No matter how I tried I could not remove the thoughts the pod triggered: cure, remission.

Can you give me one more day? I texted back to Janie.

Okay. I'll give you one more day then I've got to offer it to someone else.

Well, it seemed the pressure was on. My nurse came back with a heat pack for my arm even though they weren't supposed to – health and safety bollocks. They used microwaved bags of saline solution and I always found this amusing. She gave it to me wrapped in a couple of paper towels. I stuffed it up my sleeve, the heat soothing the pain left by the drugs.

As I trudged downstairs I remembered Janie's text of a few days earlier, telling me how the machine would ease chemo side effects. Jimmy wasn't here yet and I waited in the warmth of the reception area. To be honest, if I'd had my wits about me, I'd have felt stupid standing in the shelter of the hospital, gloves on my hands, a scarf around my neck, a winter coat buttoned up all the way on a late spring day. All of those layers because I feared the light drizzle and a gentle wind.

The thought of having what Janie described as a painless session in her machine relieve the issues the drugs gave me suddenly seemed not so strange. I guessed it didn't do anything at all, just gave a placebo effect that helped the person feel better. Before I over-thought it any further, I took off a glove and sent a text to Janie.

I don't need to think about it any longer. I want to go in the machine.

The reply came as Jimmy pulled up in the drop-off zone.

Oh my god, didn't think you'd actually say yes. I'm so pleased you want to use it! You will not regret this decision. :) I'm going away today for a week's holiday. Gill and I are celebrating my being cured with a last minute getaway. I'll be back next Wednesday. Could go on Thursday? xxx

The need to go in the machine and get some relief from the drugs suddenly seemed so urgent. I blinked away tears, borne more of frustration than anything else. I'd have to cope with the side effects for a few more days, just as I had so many times before.

That Elusive Cure

The automatic doors opened and I stepped outside, my hood up and my face buried in the layers of my scarf. Should have said yes when I was in the church. Then maybe I wouldn't be feeling so shit now.

"How are you?" Jimmy asked as I got into the car.

"Miserable."

"I've got the heat on high for you."

I glanced over. Jimmy was in a t-shirt and shorts, sweat trickling down the sides of his face as the heaters pumped out hot air.

"Thanks." I rested my hand on his leg for a moment, our eyes locked.

"It's the least I can do for you, my love."

I stared out of the window as he drove through the hospital campus. Someone dressed in a short-sleeved blouse and holding an umbrella for protection against the rain was on one of the paths. I wanted to be that person. Not afraid of the weather, huddled in a car with the heat on full, my poor Jimmy melting next to me. Next week I would be brave. I'd get in the machine and see how magic it actually was.

SIX

First Session

I arranged to be at the church at the earliest time Janie would agree to. The last week had been awful. The two days following my chemo I'd projectile vomited everything that passed through my lips. Seven days later and I was still unable to stand anything warm, so only hot liquids and hot foods would do. The exhaustion had taken me by surprise. That aspect hadn't been so bad in the previous sessions, but this past week it hit me hard, had me sleeping until noon, napping in the afternoon and in bed by eight o'clock.

All the while I suffered the side effects. The weak cough that had plagued me for months persisted. The ache in my liver ebbed and crested, sometimes sharp enough to make me gasp. Other times just a dull niggle I could easily ignore.

Each and every day I regretted not taking a chance with that blasted machine.

I arrived before Janie, parking in the tiny car park and keeping the engine running until she arrived, the heat blasting from the vents. She unlocked the door and I joined her in the church, the set up as I remembered.

"Are you excited?" she asked.

I realized my heart was beating fast, and I gave her a sheepish grin. "You know I am. I've been wishing all week I'd gone in when we came here a couple of weeks ago."

"Good. You *should* really want this. It's a privilege to be able to use this machine."

Janie placed her hand in a certain place on the hull of the pod and the lid began to open.

"How'd you do that?" I asked as I tried to work out where a switch could be located on such a smooth hull.

"It's right here. You simply place your hand there and it opens like magic." Janie kneeled and I did the same. The metal finish was smoother in the place she was pointing, but hardly noticeable and you'd only know it was there if you knew where to look. "You need to take your shoes off," she said as she glanced at my feet.

I sat on tattered red velvet steps in front of the cross and unlaced my trainers. I didn't want to ask Janie for reassurance again. Either the pod worked or it didn't. I climbed in, the funny stuff the mattress was made of expanding to cocoon me.

"What now?"

"Put your left hand on that panel above you. That'll trigger the lid."

"Okay. Here goes nothing." I took a deep breath and reached up.

The metal was cool to the touch and nothing happened for a few seconds. I half expected Janie to break out in laughter, tell me I was a fool, that this was all a hoax. But then the lid began to close slowly. A moment of panic hit me, my heart fluttering in my chest, my belly full of the collywobbles. I was about to be sealed in a fancy-looking coffin. Was I insane to agree to this?

Then a voice spoke. The voice was female. She spoke softly, reassuringly. "Please place your hand by your side."

My palm was still on that metal panel. Obediently, I lowered my arm and felt the foam envelope it, like it had the rest of my body. The lid was halfway closed now. Janie stared in, watching until the lid closed all the way and I was sealed in.

Inside the pod was more roomy than an MRI scanner, but only marginally. There was the same feeling of being straitjacketed. If something went wrong, how would I get out? Would Janie hear me shouting from the other side? How soundproofed was the pod? My stomach lurched and then I knew it, I'd vomit and asphyxiate on my breakfast because the foam wouldn't let me turn my head. These were my final moments.

Then the voice spoke again. "Heartbeat and blood pressure raised. Antihypertensive being administered."

What on earth did that mean? I hardly had time to worry. A sense of calm washed through me, the nausea disappeared and I couldn't hear my heartbeat thrumming in my chest any more.

"Patient registered via DNA. Scan initiating."

The woman's soft words relaxed me further. Could you build subliminal messages into speech? I kept my eyes closed, not wanting to restart the claustrophobic panic, and tried to detect if I could feel the machine doing anything to me.

"Diagnosing."

What would she find, I wondered. More than I already knew about?

"Eighteen tumors found in the liver ranging from 2mm to 36mm along with five seed tumors. Three tumors found in the left lung, two in the right, ranging from 18mm to 26mm along with one seed tumor in the right lung and three in the left."

Well, that was the right amount of tumors, but the idea of seed tumors was new to me, and I found the information chilling. The machine started to talk again.

"Four sessions recommended to fix cancer sites."

My eyes flashed open. That's it? Only four sessions, just like Janie! The lid of the pod didn't seem so close now, my reflection fuzzy in the brushed metal surface above me, an image of a sedate version of me that didn't show the anticipation building inside.

"Shall I begin the session?" the voice asked, and I realized I needed to respond.

"Yes…" my voice choked, the word coming out too quiet. "Yes," I repeated, this time with more confidence. This was it, this was my time, my luck, my lottery win. I had doubted Janie, dismissed the machine as madness, but here I was, encased in a magic pod expecting to be cancer free. A few weeks ago I'd been working out the best date for my funeral – one I could attend. I planned it as a celebration of my life, of life in general, and to be timed for the last weeks of my life. I liked to call it my pre-funeral. A hum built up beneath me, a kind of vibration that started at my toes and worked softly up my body. As I closed my eyes my last thought was, *this best be real*.

The vibrations concentrated on my torso for what felt like a long while. Just like Janie had said, the treatment, whatever that was, made my insides go all warm. The sensation was pleasant and if it had gone on much longer I'd probably have fallen asleep. Instead, the vibrations moved up my body to my head then stopped.

For a moment nothing happened. In the absence of the machine humming, my ears rang, making up for the sudden silence. Then the woman spoke.

"Session complete. Next session in three days' time."

When she stopped speaking, the lid popped open and slowly rose back to its original position. I felt good, as if I'd had a big dose of vitamins. I was relaxed and so comfortable I didn't even make a move to get out. The foam hugged me as I stared out the end of the pod, the cross visible again and telling me to have faith, I would be cured. God I hoped so. Not sure if it was sacrilege or some other no-no, not really sure I cared that much about offending a God who had abandoned me to cancer, but I crossed my fingers and toes and hoped for that mystical cure being offered.

"How was that?" I'd forgotten Janie was there. Startled, I felt a little of the calmness the machine had given me ebb away.

"Strange..." I thought maybe I'd have trouble extricating my body from the clinginess of the foam mattress, but as soon as I tried to pull my arms from its grip the foam deflated and flattened back down. I clambered out, slightly unsteady and holding onto Janie as she offered her arm. "Good but really strange," I said.

"How many sessions do you need?"

"Um, a few. Four I think." I frowned, trying to remember. "No, it was four. I'm sure she said I needed the same amount as you needed. You know, I was so relaxed I wasn't paying enough attention." Suddenly worried, I asked Janie, "Does it matter? Will I mess things up?"

Janie laughed. "No, I don't think it matters that much. I forgot how many days to wait before coming back and came a day late. The machine told me I was late, but it didn't seem to affect treatment in the slightest." She put the laminated card in my hands. "Here, don't forget this. It's the basics – not that it's particularly complicated. Shows you how to open the pod, climb in, place hand on lid, let it do its thing, and so on and so forth. Hold onto it and give it to the person you choose when you're done." She helped me over to a righted pew and returned to the pod, resting one hand gently on its hull.

"Am I kidding myself? Is this all a really elaborate joke?" I stared at her. "I'm not sure how much more disappointment I can take. Would you tell me if this wasn't real? Would you tell me now before I get my hopes up?"

Janie came to me and took my hands in her own. "I swear on my life that this machine works. I would never do something so cruel as pretend to have a cure. This is as real as it gets."

I nodded, seeing the honesty in her eyes. Maybe imagining it there, maybe I needed to dream for a little while. I hadn't thought of anything other than my own demise for such a long time. Everything I did seemed to be tainted by the end date hanging over my head. Even when planting the fruit trees last year I did so knowing I'd never see them grow larger than me, never see them covered in fruit. I'd never live long enough to see the asparagus crop fully. Stupid things, really. My hair would never go grey. My skin would never wrinkle. Never grow old. Never fade away. Who wants to live forever, anyway?

SEVEN

Sally Needs Help

By the time I pulled into my driveway I had decided not to tell Jimmy. He'd laugh at me, call me a fool for believing and I'd never go back for the other sessions. I'd tell him I had a nice afternoon with my new friend Janie and he'd be too busy thinking about work or in between meetings to be interested in any more details. He'd just be glad that I'd been out of the house.

Janie and I had separated on friendly terms. We'd hooked up on Facebook before driving off in separate directions, promising to keep in touch. I figured I'd be far more likely to keep that promise once I'd got proof the machine actually worked. To be honest, as I sat in my car not quite ready to go inside and face Jimmy, I began to feel a bit stupid. I thought of films about the olden days and how those quack doctors rolled up with their wagon filled with tinctures and potions and false hope, sold the promise of a cure and left before the truth could be discovered. Was I one of those gullible people waving their money in the air trying to get a bottle of snake oil before the wagon rolled off into the sunset?

But Janie hadn't asked for money. She'd given me the key, and even if she had another, it didn't stop me from passing the key onto another person. It was all so confusing and I wasn't going to solve any of this today, not here in my driveway with the sun beginning to heat the air to an unbearable level even for me. I grabbed my handbag, hiding the key to the church in the pocket where I kept a few tampons. Not that Jimmy would ever dare to go digging in my bag, he had a fear of sticking his hand in there, like he might catch something if he did.

"I'm home," I called out as I unlocked the front door and stepped inside.

Jimmy appeared at the top of the staircase, a mug in his hand. "I was just about to make tea. Want one?"

I nodded. God how I wanted a cup of tea. Curl up on the sofa with the Ray Bradbury book I was reading for the umpteenth time and forget about that stupid machine.

Jimmy stopped in the middle of the hallway, staring at me in an odd way. "What have you done? You look different."

My cheeks pinked up, how could he guess so quickly? Did that mean the machine actually did do something? "Nothing, just walking along the beach."

"That must be it." He took another long look before turning away. "Must be the sea air or catching the sun on your skin or whatever. You look almost healthy."

I laughed nervously. "Thanks," I said, attempting my best sarcastic tone and hoping he wouldn't notice.

The kettle roared into life as I collapsed onto the sofa. The day was catching up on me. I was overdue my next anti-sickness, yet the usual nausea was somehow absent.

"Did you get my messages?" Jimmy put a cup of tea on the side table next to me.

"What messages?" I dug in my handbag for my phone. Sure enough, I had a couple of messages and a missed call. I scrolled through to find Sally's name. She must have called just after I left the church.

"Sally couldn't get a hold of you. She wants to know if you can pick her kids up from school. She's having a really bad day."

"Must be to be asking for my help..." I read pretty much what Jimmy had said in her text message. I shot off a reply and glanced at the clock. "They're in an afterschool club that ends in ten minutes." I slurped at the tea. "Must go." I took one more gulp of tea, gave Jimmy a quick peck on the lips and grabbed my keys.

Peter and Lucy were waiting at the gate, a stern-looking teacher giving me her best disapproving expression as I arrived.

"Sorry I'm late," I said and herded the children back to the car before the teacher could tell me what she thought of me. She was lucky anyone was coming for them, what with their mum being a manic depressive and me with cancer. But the teacher probably didn't have a clue, Sally kept her problems as secret as possible.

The church and the machine were fading into memory by this time, like a daydream rather than being real. But the extra energy keeping me going wasn't a dream. Maybe it *was* all a placebo effect.

The kids sat quietly in the back of my car. Too quiet for eight and ten years old. I knew what they would do the minute they got home and it made me so sad. I decided to try and insert a little levity into their life and veered off the road that led to their home and went to the beach instead. When Sally and I were kids it was our favorite place to be. We'd walk the sands talking about our toys and books. Then as we got older the subject became boys and boys and... oh yes, more boys.

"Come on you two, let's go for a walk."

Lucy and Peter glanced at each other, their expressions far too adult for my liking. It was Peter who spoke. He always did, getting words out of Lucy was like finding the Holy Grail to me.

"But Mum will need us." His tone was so serious it made my heart break.

I sighed. Children his age shouldn't be worried about their mum. "She's been by herself all day. She'll be okay for another ten minutes," I told them as I engaged the handbrake.

The children exchanged another long look, the type that made me think mind reading was real. "She'll be needing me to make supper. And Lucy says she'll need a cup of tea."

I decided to ignore his pleadings and opened the door. "Just ten minutes, kids. She'll be fine."

Being an adult won the battle for me. Obedient and quiet, they climbed out of the car. I'd parked by the beach in Hoylake. Other kids were here, either with parents or without. I counted almost as many dogs as people. "We'll walk to the lifeboat station and back. The sea air will do you good."

They followed me, not once breaking into a run or smiling or chasing the puppy that came and begged for their attention. In the end I gave up halfway to the station and turned back.

We found Sally tucked up in bed. Peter went straight to the kitchen while Lucy climbed under the covers and started a whispered conversation in her mother's ear.

"Hey Sal." I sat on the armchair opposite the bed. "It's probably time to get up." I knew better than to force her. The trick was to slip in the children's needs without making her feel like a crap mother. It was a very hard trick to do.

Peter came in with a full mug. "Mum, I've put a tea beside you. Three sugars, just like you always want."

Sal was curled up on her side, the bed covers almost covering her entirely. Long strands of black hair escaped onto the pillow. They were greasy and I wondered how long it'd been since she'd had a shower.

"Peter's made a tea for you. Do you want me to put some food on for the kids?"

Sal made a small noise and buried deeper. "It's so dark," she finally said, her voice muffled by the covers.

"That's because the curtains are closed and you're buried so deep you're nearly in China." I tried to insert a joke, something to lighten the mood, if not for Sal, at least for the benefit of the kids. I opened the curtains and threw open the window. Sunlight streamed into the room, the sun low in the sky.

"That's not what I meant," Sal said.

I'd been in dark places too – maybe not like Sal, and certainly not for the same reasons – but I'd been there. Peter had gone off and reappeared with a bottle of prescription pills. He placed it next to the mug and went back to the kitchen.

I'd been taking care of Sal for as long as I could remember. Her father committed suicide when she was a baby and we spent long hours working through her emotions as teens. Then years later, Rob killed himself. I think losing her husband was harder than losing her dad in some aspects. Every day I feared what I'd find when I showed up here. Today she was still alive and I was feeling well. Almost deserved some sort of celebration. An image of the machine floated behind my eyes, reminding me of my strange afternoon. Maybe it *would* make me better. That way if Sal went further downhill… let's just say I could fulfil promises made before cancer got me.

EIGHT

Dealing with Sally

"What do you think it's like?" Sally was still under the covers. Lucy must have finished whatever it was she had to say as she crawled out from under the covers and left the room.

"What do you mean?" I knew exactly what she meant. The thing I had thought about on and off for the last two years. Would I snuff out? Be reborn in some squalling baby? Go on to a higher plane where I was rewarded for bearing the cross of cancer?

"Death." She sniffed and moved about under the covers. I guessed she was crying. "Rob came to see me earlier."

Sally laid that one out for me. Like a booby trap or landmine.

"Told me to accept the darkness. That he needed me." Sal pulled the covers back enough that I could see her face. "But the children… they need me more."

I nodded at the tea. "Peter brought you a tea and your meds."

"Would they miss me?" She glanced at the door. Fortunately the kids were elsewhere. "All day I thought about what they would do if I died. Do you think they'd cry?"

I nodded. "Of course they would. They love you very much." The last time Sal had spoken like this she'd had to go in to hospital for a few weeks. I'd looked after the kids, but that was before chemo hell took over my life. I wasn't sure I could cope right now.

"I think they'd cry. For a day or two. But then I think they would be relieved." Sal wiped the tears from her cheeks. "They'd be glad that I'd finally gone, and wasn't destroying their childhood anymore. You'd make them children again. You and Jimmy."

"Stop being silly." I sat on the side of the bed and put an arm around her. "Drink some tea. Do you want me to take out your meds?"

I waited, but she didn't reply. Her face had gone lax, the look in her eyes distant, like she was very far away.

The writing on the bottle said two. I popped the top off and put the tablets in her hand. "Here." I pushed her hand to her mouth and handed her the mug. "Swallow those down. They'll help you to feel better."

"Feel…" She was hardly even blinking. "Yes, I'd like that."

Sal swallowed the pills and a small amount of worry left me. I couldn't stay at her house forever, but I needed to make sure she was okay enough to leave her alone with the kids. I stared at her for a long while. She'd gone blank, not speaking, hardly even blinking. There was only one choice for me. I stepped out of the room and rang home.

That Elusive Cure

"Hey what's up?" Jimmy answered on the second ring.

"Sal's in a bad way. I think I'm going to have to stay the night." I peeked in the kitchen. Peter had taken out chips and fish fingers and put them on a baking tray. The oven was heating up.

"You sure you're up to that? You're not even a week out of chemo." He'd stopped typing and was listening properly, a sure sign of concern.

"Sal's in there alternating between comatose and crying while she talks about dying." The kids were in the living room watching cartoons. They were as lively as their mother. My heart ached for them.

"Maybe she needs to be somewhere else, where there are professionals who know what they're doing."

I sighed. "I can't do that to her. What about the kids? A half-working Sally is better than a foster home. I guarantee it. I can't cope with them full-time right now - maybe in a few weeks when I've recovered from the last cycle. I'm getting a break, the docs said they'd give me three months to recuperate, I could look after them then... if Sal can just hold on a little longer."

"We can't have the kids. Are you an idiot? How are you supposed to get better if instead of resting you're looking after a couple of kids?"

Still thinking I had a chance of getting better. Poor Jimmy. He was as deluded as Sal. I was going to slowly get worse until they gave me morphine and called time on my treatment.

"Look, I'm staying the night, and that's that. You know where I am." I hung up, staring at the phone for a minute, willing Jimmy to ring back, tell me he loved me and supported me, but the phone remained silent.

I stood in the hallway, torn for a moment as to who to go to first. The familiar dull ache had started up in my liver. So much for my magic machine. I decided to go to the kids, tell them their Auntie Kathy was staying the night, but the tears took me by surprise before I had the chance. For a long time I stood in the hall sobbing. Crying for Sally, for her kids, for the life that was being stolen from me, for the life Sal didn't want, but mostly for the machine that was never going to save me.

Sal stayed in bed all evening, leaving me to concentrate on the kids. Thank God I had this mystery boon of energy – whether placebo or actual – it was welcome and frankly necessary. I got the kids off to school the next morning and after waiting to what I judged to be the reasonable hour of ten o'clock, I ventured into Sal's bedroom bearing a tray of toast and orange juice.

"Come on, you. Time to shake the funk off." I opened the curtains and sat in the arm chair. I felt like I was on a repeat of the day before.

It was a few minutes before Sal even moved. I'd almost nodded off as well, her rhythmic deep breaths sending me towards a nap.

"It's not a funk." No hello, no good morning, no how are my kids today. But I hadn't expected any of that. I'd prodded her on purpose. Years of dealing with her had given me tools to help. Sal's sister used to come around more and when Sal got like this Wendy would use the kids and throw a guilt trip on

Sal about her lack of mothering skills. All that did was send Sal even further down the rabbit hole. The best way, at least for now, was to make her defensive. Not angry, just defensive. It was a knife's edge. Get her too angry, and I'd be cleaning up a destroyed house after she went on a rampage.

"Yes Sal. You're in a funk."

"It's not a fucking funk. Stop being a bitch."

I shrugged. "Suit yourself." I went to the kitchen and boiled the kettle, getting the meds she needed ready as the tea brewed. "Here." I was back in her bedroom. I put the mug of tea on the side along with her tablets. "As it's not a funk you need your meds."

Sally gave me a dirty look, but I'd made my point and she took the pills without argument.

"You getting up today?"

Her bed was a mess, the sheet half off so she was lying on the mattress. The whole room stank of stale, sweaty human. The open window simply wasn't helping enough.

"We could go for a walk down by the beach." I got up and stared down her garden. The grass needed mowing and the patio was almost hidden by the weeds growing in the cracks.

She wasn't biting. Sally had thrown the bed covers over her head and was lying perfectly still. Playing dead. The phrase popped into my mind and stuck. Seemed horribly appropriate given what was probably going through her mind.

"We could have a joint funeral."

Finally. Words. I'd all but given up.

"I'm not planning on going anytime soon. So I guess you won't be either. Best get out of bed and try to live a little before the end." I was impatient. In the back of my mind, the pod teased me, distracted me. I needed to be there for Sal, completely, not with my mind still in a filthy old church in Birkenhead.

"It's easy for you to say. I have this darkness on me. It's like an oily blanket and I can't get out from underneath."

"You should try a wash then." I regretted the words the minute they left my mouth.

I heard a sound and realized she had started weeping. "Don't you think I would if it was that easy? Everything is so hard. Moving is hard. Eating is hard. Feeling is hard. I keep thinking it would be easier if I just snuffed out, but with you being ill I don't know what would happen to the kids, and it's the only thing keeping me here right now."

I couldn't cope today. All the words I wanted to say were geared to hurt, to dig, to force her into action, any action. Sal had gone emotionless again. She'd sat up in bed, tears drying on her cheeks. Morning had gone, the afternoon bringing the sun. I watched as the light crept across the carpet. Jimmy had rung, telling me he loved me, just like I'd wanted but inside I felt as numb as Sally did. I felt like I was here for duty, not love like I normally was. The ache in my liver wasn't so bad, less than it had been a week ago. I told Jimmy who said thank God the chemo was working. The business with the pod had built up inside me. I wanted to confess, to tell Jimmy what I'd done, where I'd gone. I didn't care if he called me insane. But I didn't, I kept it quiet and told Jimmy I thought I might come home today.

That Elusive Cure

School leaving time, and I still hadn't got Sal to move. I picked up the kids, their disappointment in seeing me painful to bear. My patience at an end, for a moment I thought maybe I should call in the professionals, but my feet were too fast, and suddenly there I was, standing at the end of her bed, hands on hips.

"Enough wallowing!" I shouted at her.

Sally all but fell out of bed in surprise.

"You've got two kids out there who hated that I picked them up from school. They love you and need you. I've got an ache in my belly that needs my pain pills and I'm too afraid to leave you and go get them. You're being selfish holed up in bed and refusing to move. Either get moving or I'm calling for back up."

"Bitch," she spat the words at me. "You're no better than Wendy."

That hurt, but I wasn't backing down. I'd pandered to her and that hadn't worked. "I can bugger off if you like. Let your little boy play carer. Is that what you want?"

"Why are you being such a *bitch* to me?"

"Because look at us. The sick looking after the sick. Jimmy wants me home so I can rest. He still thinks I'm going to get better, and that weighs on me, it bloody crushes me. I'm never getting better. I'm on the slow road to death. I don't get an option. I had plans to live to one hundred years old. I was going to celebrate my centennial with a book about all the big changes in the world during my life. Instead I'll be lucky if I see forty-five. And then there's you, with a perfectly good body wishing yourself dead. Do you know how jealous I am of you?" There, it had come out. The words I'd never intended to share.

The kids had heard the shouting and were standing in the hall outside the bedroom door. Christ, they did not need to hear this.

"I'd swap bodies with you if I could. In a heartbeat."

Her words triggered a wave of shame. My anger disappeared in an instant. "Oh Sally, I'm so sorry." I sat on the edge of the bed. "I shouldn't have said those things."

"I don't want to go to the headcase hotel." Sal didn't tear up, she didn't frown, or stare wide-eyed and knowingly at me. Her face didn't give away any emotion. She simply lay there staring at me, her expression bland.

"I won't let them section you again." I touched her arm, unsure if she was ready for human contact.

Sally nodded at me, the first proper emotions breaking through, her eyes glassy as she put her hand over mine. We stayed like that for a long time. I knew she'd get through this episode when she finally got up out of that bed and went to the shower.

As I changed her bed clothes, self-loathing came over me. Instead of thinking about Sally and her kids, and the breakthrough I'd made in simply getting her to wash, my mind was fixed on that damn machine and how I'd get another session in two days. Sally was right. I was a bitch.

NINE

Second Session

After judging Sally safe enough to allow me to make a run home, I gathered my medicines and a change of clothing and stayed one more night. The next morning I left Sal as she stood in the kitchen trying to work out what to make for lunch, with the kids in front of the telly watching the Saturday cartoons. Exhaustion was catching up with me. This was proper chemo exhaustion. The type that turned me into the walking dead.

I got back home and dropped my overnight bag, shoes and coat as I walked up stairs. The scattered trail would tell Jimmy where I was because I hadn't the energy left to even speak. I was lucky to have managed the drive home at all.

The rest of the day passed in a haze. Fall into bed. Get up, use the loo. Drink the tea Jimmy left for me. Turn the telly on and close my eyes because watching the television hurt them. Doze, fade in and out of scattered conversations as Jimmy checked up on me. Ignore the anger in his voice when he mentioned Sal. Change into pajamas as the night draws in. Sniff at the soup Jimmy brings and sit up long enough to drink it before falling unconscious again. Feel the kiss placed lightly on my lips as he climbs under the covers. Then night came again and a darker, denser sleep took me, a chemo sleep.

I woke on Sunday feeling better, but still tired. It wasn't until almost noon that I remembered the machine and that I was due my second session. Butterflies alighted in my stomach. Jimmy was in his study, probably on his computer scanning the headlines. Somehow I needed to get away from him and to the church. Janie had said a day late didn't matter, but a need grew in me, almost as if my body believed in the cure more than my mind. To get away from Jimmy on a Sunday would take planning.

"I'm having a quick shower then I'm off to my mum's for a cup of tea." The lie slid out far too easily.

"You sure you're up for that?" he called out from his study. "Maybe you should cancel. Why can't you see her tomorrow?"

"I promised her. Dad's away on one of his old-boys' weekends. She's all by herself."

Not wanting to hear any more reasons as to why I shouldn't go, I locked myself in the bathroom and had a quick shower. Jimmy was still in his study as I came out. Minutes later I was dressed and tiptoeing down the stairs. I grabbed my key to the church and handbag as I called up to him, "See you in a couple of hours, I won't be long." I didn't wait for his reply and ran out the door.

Twenty minutes later I pulled up into the tiny car park beside the church. The key was in my hand already, my palm damp with anticipation. The day was warm, and the streets busy with people. I tried not to look conspicuous as I got out of the car and slipped the key into the lock. The key wouldn't turn. I took it out and pushed it back in, rattling the doorknob and turning the key harder. Still nothing. Then I remembered Janie's advice about jiggling the key. A moment later I was inside the church.

I'd half expected the machine to be gone, that I'd find it had never existed. But there it was, in the middle of the room, at odds with the dirt and dust coating everything else in there. The machine stood out, shiny and new-looking.

Wasting no time, I sat on one of the few righted pews and took off my shoes, leaving my handbag on the seat. The pod called to me and I could believe it was going to cure me. Even if it didn't, would it hurt me so much to believe just for a little while? To have a few days where I felt like I might make it through this, that the rest of my days on this earth wouldn't be filled with treatments and drugs?

The foam grew around me and I lay down, my hand already placed on the pad in the lid. My heartbeat quickened as the lid eased down. I wasn't scared this time, I was *excited*. A possible future was growing before me, and I couldn't feel better about it.

"Patient recognized. Heartbeat and blood pressure raised. Antihypertensive being administered."

Fine, not a problem. Excitement built in me. Two more sessions after this I'd be whole again. No more cancer beasties eating me from the inside out. The machine did its thing and I felt my heartbeat calm.

"Scan initiating."

Initiate away, I thought. It was probably for the best that I was alone and enclosed in the pod as I was sure the smile of a lunatic was pasted across my face. Maybe I was more tuned in, but this time I felt a slight sensation beneath me. It reminded me of a much more advanced version of an MRI scanner.

"Diagnosing."

The smile on my face dulled as I waited for the results. Would it be the same as three days ago? Could more tumors have grown in that time? My liver had begun to ache again, and that just couldn't be a good thing. What if the machine said I had some completely different illness? Could be the first time was a fluke or really was set up by Janie. I tried to dismiss the doubts, but two years of the cancer journey had taught me never to expect the best case scenario. It was simply too painful when the news didn't live up to the hope. And the news *never* lived up to the hope.

The female voice began speaking again, "Thirteen tumors found in the liver ranging from 1mm to 30mm. Two tumors found in the left lung, one in the right ranging from 9mm to 14mm."

That was a huge change from the last scan. Amazing! I wanted to escape the pod and dance about the church. Scream and shout and holler, kick up the dust and celebrate how good life can be when it wants to.

"Heartbeat and blood pressure raised. Antihypertensive being administered."

The antidote or whatever it was really got me this time. The need to run about eased and suddenly I was close to sleep.

"Session two of the four recommended."

I breathed deeply. Calmer by the second. I allowed myself to restore a little more faith in the machine.

"Shall I begin the session?" the voice asked me.

I was ready for the question this time. "Yes," I said and relaxed into the foam, waiting for the machine to work.

Vibrations started at my feet like before, working their way along my body until the pod was still once more.

"Session complete. Next session in three days' time."

The lid opened and I lay there a while, not moving from the pod, comfortable and close to sleep.

"What the hell do you think you're doing?" A man's voice came from somewhere behind me.

I leapt from the machine. I'd forgotten to lock the door! Oh my God, a rapist or a murderer could be in here with me. How could I be so stupid as to forget to lock the frigging door behind me? I spun around and tripped backwards into a pile of pews. The back of my skull bashed against one of the benches and silver stars rained down, blurring my vision. The man was coming over, and my body wouldn't move, wouldn't obey my desperate orders to flee.

"No, please. Don't hurt me."

The man came into focus as he loomed over me, and I knew him.

"Jimmy?" I said, and then fainted.

I came to in the pod. Jimmy must have picked me up and put me there. He was sitting on a pew he'd dragged nearer to the machine.

"Kath?" Jimmy jumped up and came over. "You've been out for a couple of minutes. Any longer and I was going to call for an ambulance." He stroked my head gently. "See if you can sit up."

I did as he said, the back of my skull tender to the touch, but not too painful. "I'm okay, really," I said as he stared intently into each of my eyes.

"How many fingers do you see?" He held two fingers up.

"I'm fine, Jimmy."

He backed off, giving me a little space while I stood up. Thinking better of it, I sat down again.

"So what the hell is this?"

Here it comes, all the questions. I shrugged and rubbed the back of my head. Truth was, my thoughts were a bit jumbled from the bump. I couldn't think up a story that might satisfy him when I couldn't even string two thoughts together.

"Come on, Kath." He slapped the machine. "What is this, a tanning booth? Why would you have it here? And what about the church? Are you taking out loans I don't know about?"

"It's not a tanning booth."

"How much debt have you racked up? Don't you think I do enough for you already?" He walked around the machine.

I didn't know what to say. Shame filled me. How could I not have told Jimmy? I should have been honest with him from the start.

That Elusive Cure

"If I hadn't needed some things from the hardware store I wouldn't have been this end of town and would never have seen your car." He paced back and forth, kicking up dust.

"I'm sorry. I didn't say anything because I thought you'd tease me and call me a fool."

That made him stop. "What are you talking about?"

"The machine, this thing." I ran my hand slowly over the smooth metal. "My new friend Janie, she showed it to me and gave me the key to the church. It's from the future or something. It fixed her, made her cancer go away."

Jimmy sat down on the pew and put his head in his hands. "And you think this machine will do the same to you." He didn't sound angry anymore, just so, so sad.

"I just had my second session and something is happening, I swear. My liver aches so much less. I can't even feel it right now. It scans me and tells me the size of my tumors, they've reduced so much."

"Oh, Kath. You can't let yourself believe this. It's a fairy tale, a joke this woman is playing on you." Jimmy knelt in front of me and took my hands. "When you get your next scan and you find out nothing has changed, you'll be devastated. Do you remember when they cancelled your surgery last year? Do you remember how bad you got?"

How could I forget. The liver consultant was going to operate on my liver and then I'd be free of stupid cancer. But they'd grown and multiplied between scans. I went into hospital that morning for the operation, changed into a hospital gown, hair in a special net, all my jewelry off, my feet in those throwaway shoe covers, and those tight stockings on my legs. The doctor was late, and when he showed up told me I'd gone from operable to inoperable, then left me on my own as I began to sob. The weeks afterwards were among the darkest I've ever lived through.

I nodded at Jimmy. "But I feel it working."

"Kath…"

"No, Jimmy. You told me to do whatever was necessary. This machine feels necessary. Even if it doesn't fix me, at least I'll have had a few weeks of the dream, because if this doesn't work then the alternative is simply to wait until the end." I felt a tear slip down my cheek. "All of this freaking sucks. I *hate* it. I *hate* it. I *hate* it. I've tried your ideas, eating low carb until my breath stinks, then the juicing detox that lasted weeks. Total avoidance of sugars and processed meats. All those vitamins that each suggest they might help my odds. I've HATED it. I just wanted to be normal. But I did it all for you because you hoped it would fix me or help or something. Well this time *I* want to do something that *I* think might help. And what the hell do *I* have to lose?"

"Nothing," Jimmy said. He pulled me close and wrapped his arms around me. We sat that way for a long time, our sobs the only sound.

TEN

Cake and Hope

The next few days passed in a blur. Jimmy apologized so many times I had to tell him I'd hit him if he said sorry one more time. He talked about how I should have been able to tell him about the pod from the beginning, about how he'd forced all those quack and not so quack remedies on me without any thought of what I wanted. I could only take so much. Of course I wanted the same as him. I'd take the potential cures, whether I thought they were foolish or not. I wanted to live. And not this hazy chemo existence. A normal life with normal struggles, a chance to go grey and wrinkly, time given so I could see any grandchildren Cass might produce.

We'd seen her, she'd come over Monday night with that tattooed boyfriend of hers and all I could think was how obvious it was that Cass and Jack loved each other, how tenderly he took care of her. Then the darkness descended as I wondered if they'd ever get married and would it be before I died.

I sighed, a long sigh that seemed to go on forever and wished the sadness in me would hitch a ride and go away forever.

Summer had finally come and I was outside in the hammock. The docs said I wasn't supposed to get too much sun when on chemo. The meds make your skin hypersensitive or something. I long ago stopped listening. How many things can you have taken from you before you rebel? Apparently sunbathing was my tipping point. So here I was, in the hammock in a little t-shirt and my leggings pulled up to expose my legs.

My book had dropped to the grass. I had too much on my mind to concentrate on the story. Sal had called. She needed me to go around. I was avoiding just a little bit longer. I needed to be alone, to try and find peace in the rays of sun. I was due my third session in the machine tomorrow. Jimmy wanted to come with me to see what happened from start to finish. I felt vaguely crowded by his request and didn't know why.

Maybe because it *was* all bollocks. I was in one of those moods. Expect nothing, hope for nothing and then you can't be disappointed when it all goes wrong. I didn't want Jimmy there because I didn't want him finding out the pod was all a clever trick and informing me afterwards about how it really was fake and that I was as poorly as ever.

Bollocks. Why couldn't *normal* be the path laid out for me? Or if cancer had to be part of my life plan then make it be found early on. Not when it's sent out seeds and the docs don't stand a chance.

Bollocks. I wasn't going to miraculously start to relax. Time for the depressed to help the clinically depressed. That should be fun. Sal and I could score points off each other, see who had the bigger tale of woe. Drink tea and eat the cakes that I wasn't supposed to, reminding each other that Jimmy couldn't know. Passing time as tomorrow was taking forever to come.

Janie had messaged me on Facebook this morning. Asked if I was beginning to notice a difference. I hadn't replied yet, but the fact was when Cass had shown up last night, first thing she did was tell me how well I looked. She'd been so taken by my change in appearance that she'd put on the hall light and turned me this way and that. Told me that my eyes didn't have that sick, slightly yellow look about them. How the spots the chemo caused had almost gone, and that if she didn't know better, she'd never have guessed I had cancer.

Bollocks. Who was I kidding. Someone with a sick sense of humor had got that pod off eBay. It was probably a Star Trek prop and they'd set up a tape to play and a motor to close and open the lid. I should look for the hidden cameras in the church. Give them the finger and bash up their 'machine'.

And yet, despite everything common sense told me, I couldn't wait to go back for my next session.

Enough stupid thinking. It got me nowhere but more depressed. I rolled off the hammock and made my way to Sal's house.

"Have it. Have the cake."

Sally had been busy. In an effort to try and pull herself out of the pits (as she called it) she'd started baking. She cut a large slice of chocolate cake and handed it to me.

"Jimmy won't have a clue. It'll be our secret."

The cake was three layers with chocolate frosting and what looked like Minstrels decorating the top. How could I say to no to such an effort?

"The garden's still a mess, but I'm sure that won't bother you."

I grabbed my cup of tea and shook my head. "Better for the bees, right?"

"I wish the landlord felt that way."

Sal had a long garden, most of it overgrown. Flowers from a couple of enormous, scraggly bushes gave a secret garden feeling. Like somehow back here we were hidden not only from the neighbors, but the world in general and all those bad things that were always trying to get at us.

"Use this, Kath." Sal tossed a damp tea towel at me and I wiped the patio chairs down, chasing away spiders and getting most of the bird splots off.

We settled down, neither of us speaking for a moment while we ate the cake.

"My sister found out I've been down again." Sal didn't look at me, but stared down the garden. For a moment I thought she'd forgotten I was there and that she was talking to herself. "That's what finally made me pull myself together. You threaten to section me. She actually would."

I listened, unsure what to say.

That Elusive Cure

"Sorry about calling you a bitch. You're my best friend. You know that, right?" Sally turned to me, a bright smile on her face. I knew it to be paint, a fake, a Mona Lisa smile. She was still down there, fighting the shadow monsters, but at least she was fighting. Last week she was letting them feed on her, and this was what I called progress.

"No worries. That's what I'm here for. You know that."

We supped our tea and watched the birds dip in and out of the garden chasing insects.

"You're different somehow, but I can't quite put my finger on how."

My heart did a little skip.

"It's almost as if you're not sick. That would be wonderful, wouldn't it?" Sally finished her tea and the conversation in the same moment. "You've got chocolate down your front. You'll never get that past Jimmy without him guessing you've eaten something you shouldn't."

"Shit." I looked down to find a blob of frosting on my white top. Sugar was the big thing Jimmy preached against. Sugar fed cancer. Break down all my favorite foods and you got glucose. For nearly two years I'd been sneaking treats behind Jimmy's back. I was getting tired of it to be honest. Yet despite this, I still went inside to attack the stain with cleaner.

Looking around the house, I could see how bad things had got with Sal. She didn't need threats of being put away in the madhouse, she needed someone to roll up their sleeves and lend a hand. After a moment of indecision I decided to start with the bathroom. Sal was out in the garden still. She'd probably not even notice I'd gone and not come back. She'd be off in her own world again, chatting quietly to the garden as if I was still there.

As I scrubbed the floor I allowed the fantasy of the cure to play out. Three people had now noticed a difference in me. If everything went according to the plan of the machine, with three days between treatments, I could expect to be cured in four days. My heart skipped a beat. *Four days?* Such a short amount of time, I hadn't thought about it like that before. Four days to be fixed, to be normal again. I allowed a silly grin to spread across my face. Cured. Remission. Words that might soon apply to me. I moved on to cleaning the toilet, whistling as I worked.

ELEVEN

Third Session

I woke up Wednesday morning to find Jimmy out of bed, showered and in his study answering emails. Moments after he realized I was awake, he came in. He looked anxious, nervous as he sat on the side of the bed and fiddled with a pen.

"Today's the day."

"Third session. It's so quick," I said. "You sure you want to come?"

He nodded. "Try and stop me."

"I'm not sure what you'll hear on the outside. The computer speaks quietly."

"Do you really think it's working?" Jimmy took my hand. "Don't you think we should prepare in case this is all a hoax?"

"You do what you want. I'll deal with the reality after the next MRI scan."

Jimmy looked like he was going to say more, but got to his feet instead. "I'll get you some tea," he said as he left the room.

I got ready slowly. Part of me never wanted to go back to that church. My insides felt all mixed up. I wanted to be cured, who wouldn't? But the truth was I was setting myself up for a big dose of the painful truth and didn't seem to be able to stop myself from travelling the path. It sucked.

I moved around the house like a ghost until finally I stood by the front door, that big old key in one hand and Jimmy at my side. I placed my other hand lightly on his arm. I didn't say anything, just stared up at him. I didn't need to say anything. We were both fighting the same emotions.

"Come on, let's go." Jimmy moved past me and out to the car. I wondered how we'd cope, after the scan and the inevitable let down. And yet I climbed in next to him and off we drove.

We entered the church, and there it was; the machine as shiny and at odds with the surroundings as ever. Jimmy ran his fingers over the metal hull while I struggled with the lock. No way was I making that mistake twice. I rattled the handle to make sure we were indeed locked in before making my way over to Jimmy.

I touched the hidden panel and the lid opened.

"Have a feel of the mattress. It's really odd."

Jimmy touched the material tentatively, pulling back suddenly as the foam tried to grab on. "What the hell…?"

I laughed. "Weird, huh?"

"It grows?"

"Is it getting harder to believe this thing is fake?" I asked as I sat on a pew and took off my shoes.

"Yes…" He prodded the mattress, a faint smile on his lips as the foam reacted.

I climbed in and lay down. "Now don't be going anywhere, you hear?"

He let out a short laugh, watching me closely, watching the machine, watching the foam mattress as it snugged up around my body, his eyes trying to be everywhere at once.

"See you on the other side," I said as I reached up and placed my palm on the panel. The lid began to move, slowly and smoothly closing me in, Jimmy's eyes on mine until the lid clicked shut.

I shifted a little, getting comfortable, the foam adjusting along with me.

The machine started to speak, "Patient recognized. Scan initiating."

Apparently my heartbeat and blood pressure weren't raised this time. I had to admit I didn't feel as anxious or scared in the pod today. Last time I was in the MRI at Clatterbridge Hospital the nurses had to tell me not to be so relaxed as I was breathing too slowly. Maybe I was getting the same way with this machine. The lid would lift up and Jimmy would find me fast asleep.

"Diagnosing."

A moment of truth, if the machine was to be believed.

"Seven tumors found in the liver ranging from 3mm to 25mm. One tumor found in the left lung measuring 3mm, right lung now clear."

I couldn't help but let the excitement grow in me. Right lung clear. Did she really say my right lung was clear? I almost shouted out to Jimmy to ask if he'd heard the machine speaking, but then she started again.

"Session three of the four recommended."

Time would show Jimmy and me if these sessions were real or a painfully disappointing waste of time.

"Shall I begin the session?" the machine asked.

"Yes," I said and waited for the thing to get going.

As the vibrations moved along my body, I wondered what Jimmy could hear. Did he have a hand on the hull, did he feel the machine working, doing whatever it was that it did? My torso went quite warm as the vibrations concentrated on that area. Maybe it used some sort of futuristic nanotechnology, or magnets, or some method I'd never heard of and hadn't even been invented yet. I really did lean towards the theory that the pod was from the future.

The machine stopped. "Session complete. Next session in three days' time."

The lid opened and Jimmy was waiting right there, and he looked far too excited.

"I heard it, I heard what it said!" He held out a hand and helped me out of the machine. Before I even had a chance to get my balance he had wrapped me up in a bear hug.

"You heard?"

"Every word. There's a speaker on the outside. Everything you heard, I heard."

I smiled shyly. "Do you think I should believe then? Get my hopes up?"

"Makes me want to pay for a private CT scan and see what they make of your insides." He kissed me hard on the lips. "Your right lung is clear? That's amazing."

"Don't count your chickens. Remember you were telling *me* to calm down about this not so long ago."

My phone beeped and I peeled myself out of Jimmy's arms. I sat on the pew and read the message – Janie.

Is today your next session? I hope you're feeling some relief from the pain by now and are starting to believe. It's a miracle, isn't it?

"It's Janie again. I should have replied to her the other day." At that moment I realized I couldn't remember the last time I felt an ache in my liver. One day? Or maybe it was two. Could a placebo take away my pain? I seriously doubted that when some days the morphine the docs prescribed didn't even touch the pain.

Jimmy wasn't listening. He was circling the machine, examining it.

Yes, I just finished my third session. My pains seem to have gone.

Unsure of what else to say, I sent the message. A reply came quickly.

I'm so pleased for you. Next session on Saturday?

A small part of me wanted to lie, to hide my schedule from her. Despite her sharing this machine with me, she really was still a stranger.

Yes.

"I found it." Jimmy was on the far side of the pod, out of sight. I put my phone down and went over to him.

"Found what?"

"The engine compartment."

He'd managed to find an opening where I hadn't seen one and opened it. A two meter by half a meter panel had slid down into the bottom of the pod. What was visible looked like the engine of a new car. The machinery was packed in tight, with hardly enough room to squeeze a hand or tool.

"Pretty amazing, isn't it?" Jimmy reached out to touch the parts.

"No, don't do a thing!" I knocked his arm out of the way. "What if you do something and you break it?"

"I'm not a complete idiot, you know." His sulking face was on now, and for a moment I thought he was going to ignore me and have a poke around inside anyway. Then he pulled gently on the panel and it slid back into place. The seal was near invisible.

"Beautiful, isn't it." Jimmy stroked the hull.

"Come on, time to go." I was afraid Jimmy couldn't resist having a tinker. He loved figuring out how things worked and now that he knew a way in to the engine, I wanted to keep him away.

I slipped my shoes back on and grabbed my bag. "Let's go." I took his hand and pulled him away. His eyes followed too closely when I hid the key in my bag. Before he'd even started the car I knew I'd have to find a new hiding place.

"With a bit of time, I'm sure I could figure out how that thing works." He muttered the words, as if half to me, and half to himself.

A chill came over me. Yes, I definitely had to hide the key.

TWELVE

Chemo Day

Thursday was a chemo day. I woke up apprehensive, a part of me trying to convince the rest of me that I didn't need to go. But there was no chance of giving up traditional treatment. That would be just stupid. For a brief moment I thought about ringing up the hospital and saying I'd had a really hard time with the side effects and needed a week off. This was the last session before the next break between courses of chemotherapy. That meant in less than two weeks I'd get a CT scan or an MRI, depending on what the doctor wanted. Then I would find out the truth, find out if Janie was right or if I was a fool.

I wanted the drive to Clatterbridge to be silent. I wanted to be left alone with my thoughts. But Jimmy prattled on beside me, hardly pausing for breath. He'd spent the early morning researching medical machinery and trying to find similarities between what already existed and what he'd seen inside the pod. Turns out he'd taken pictures on his phone for reference.

The key to the church was hidden safely away, or so I hoped. I'd hidden it at the bottom of a box of tampons. Not that I needed them anymore. The medicines long ago put paid to my fertility. I hoped when Jimmy went searching, and I knew he would, that he wouldn't think to look there.

My phone beeped. I'd been sitting with my head tilted away from Jimmy. He didn't even realize I wasn't listening. I'd been watching the trees whip past the window as we drove along the motorway. I glanced at the screen. Janie had messaged me.

Are you going to get your chemo today?

I wondered how close she came to jacking it all in when she was getting treatment at the hospital and visiting the pod within days of each other.

I am, heading there now.

"...I found a picture of a new style scanner they are developing in Massachusetts at some hospital there." Jimmy looked more animated and happy than I had seen him in ages. "The mechanisms in that are remarkably similar to the ones in the *MicroHealth* machine maybe..."

I tuned Jimmy out again as my phone beeped. Janie had responded.

I kept going as well. No point risking buggering up the chemo, just in case. That's what I figured. Belts and braces, lol.

Jimmy pulled off the motorway and onto the exit ramp, still talking away. "...They're also developing nanotechnology with some success. I can't find pictures of how they're making that happen, I'm guessing they've got the designs under lock and key..."

That Elusive Cure

I typed in a reply. *Feels strange going in. Like an exercise in futility. I suppose it can't hurt, but I have to admit I feel so well. Over the last year I'd started to feel like a proper cancer patient. I realized this morning that I'm not thinking like that anymore.*

Jimmy drove into the hospital complex and up to the security guard's kiosk. He wound the window down. "Bringing her in for treatment," he said to the guard.

The gate lifted and we drove in. Last day of treatment? Last day of burning veins? Last day of sickness and a long list of side effects that came hand-in-hand with the medicines? Butterflies erupted in my belly and I realized just how desperate I was for this elusive cure.

Be real, I thought, picturing the pod, the sinky foam mattress and the warm feeling in my guts as the machine did whatever it did. *Be real*.

As usual there were a few people milling about near the entrance to the oncology ward. I couldn't figure them out. Patients wheeled their drips out with them, dressed in pajamas and dressing gowns, or pushed out by enablers in their wheelchairs, all so they could have a stupid smoke. Most of them were gaunt, end stage patients, their skin as grey as the ash on their cigarette, cheekbones sticking out as they inhaled. And they made me *so* angry.

I wanted to go up to each of them, give them a shake and shout, "Do you think this helps?" If I could do something to make my bowel cancer better, increase my odds, I'd do it in a heartbeat. If I'd been a smoker I'd have given it up the day I was diagnosed.

I'd given up processed foods, wheat, dairy, and the sweetest fruits. For over a year I gave up sugar until I started to cheat and sneak the occasional cake back into my diet. Even discounting the sugar issues, virtually everything that passed my lips was organic. It had got to the point where it seemed there was little I *could* eat. Did I like doing this? Absolutely not. I was sick of not eating like a normal person. I missed ice cream and chocolate and bread and scones and a hundred other things. But I avoided them for a reason, for the slight chance, the possibility, the *maybe* that eliminating them might increase my odds.

The smokers made me so angry, yet I tried my best to hide it as I walked past.

"You're so bloody judgmental," Jimmy said once we were inside.

I flashed him my disapproving look and stalked off towards the stairs. I ascended fast, realizing on the half landing that my knees weren't hurting in the slightest. I forgot my irritation at Jimmy and turned to him, smiling.

"The pain's gone."

"What pain?"

"The ache in my joints that the steroids give me. It's all gone." The grin was stretching across my face. I strode into the waiting room, looking far too happy to be there, and reported in at the reception desk.

"Are you seeing the doctor today?" The receptionist asked.

"Nope, I don't think so, but it's my last treatment." I glanced at Jimmy and added, "For now." I shouldn't play with the fates and jinx things before I knew I was being fixed for certain.

The wait was as long as ever. Over an hour of sitting quietly. Jimmy kept his mouth shut, even though I could see he was itching to talk about the gubbins of the pod and instead spent the time surfing the web on his phone. No doubt researching about nanotechnology some more.

Me, I spent the hour people watching. I knew what I was doing. I was choosing who I would send to the machine once I had been fixed.

"Kathy Wyatt." A nurse came into the waiting room calling my name.

"One more time?" I asked Jimmy quietly.

He shrugged. "Who knows. But I'm beginning to have faith."

Jimmy? Finding the faith? Maybe it *was* time to believe just a little bit.

The nurse showed me through to Bay 3, the littlest one with only three treatment chairs. Jimmy pulled up a seat and sat next to me while the nurse busied herself with checking my medicines.

"Can you take these, please." Julie placed a small paper cup with seven pills in the bottom and went to get some water for me. I poked the pills, not entirely sure what they were, and realizing I'd never bothered to ask. I thought the two small round white ones were steroids and the others were a couple of different types of anti-sickness. But like I said, I wasn't really sure.

"Can you confirm name and date of birth?"

I repeated these several times as she went through the bags of IV solution for today and packets of pills for the next nine days, doing the last check before hooking me up. Then it was time, the part I hated the most, the needle in the back of the hand. You'd think I'd be used to them by now. Two years of being poked by people. I had dimpled scars from needles in the crooks of my arms and the backs of my hands. I watched as she prepared everything and looked away as she got ready to pierce my skin.

"Ouch," I said, my body stiffening, but somehow keeping my hand perfectly still. It was a practiced expression of pain.

"I'm just going to give it a flush through, and then we're all set to begin."

Nurse Julie walked off, letting the flush run. And all I could think was: *the pod doesn't hurt*.

THIRTEEN

Feeling... normal

Friday morning arrived, and I did a surprising thing – I woke up. Usually the day after chemo was the first of a week of late sleeps and feeling dreadful. Instead... I sat up and almost felt the need to pinch myself. I felt normal.

My mobile beeped, Janie had texted.

How are you feeling today, are you up to a visitor?

I stared for a moment. I was not up to a visitor, I decided, at least not at home.

No, but do you fancy going out? I feel the need for doing something different.

A reply came seconds later.

What are you thinking?

I wasn't sure. I didn't want to hang around the sick house, not when I was feeling so good. Feeling, dare I say it, normal.

What about out, tonight?

I had a bucket list somewhere. Jimmy had told me to write it out almost two years ago when we first got the diagnosis. Problem with bucket lists is I kind of see it as a celebration of me being sick, a reward. And

I certainly didn't want to think of a weekend away somewhere nice as a prize for getting ill. So the list had been put away, collecting dust until I got really ill and couldn't manage the things anymore.

Before Janie had a chance to reply, I knew what it was I wanted. *Pub crawl?*

A good five minutes passed before a reply came. I figured maybe she was a teetotaler and I'd just offended her or something. Then my phone beeped.

You're on.

Excellent. I climbed out of bed and headed for Jimmy's study. "I'm off out tonight. Girls' night."

Jimmy pushed back from his desk and stared at me. "You sure that's a wise idea?"

"I feel great!" I dropped into the armchair in the corner of the room. "Really, I don't feel like the chemo has given me a single side effect."

Jimmy got up and took one of his guitars from where they hung on the wall. He idly strummed for a moment then said. "I can't think of a better advert for that machine. Every home should have one." He gave me a big goofy grin. "Go on, have fun. Have a drink and let your hair down."

Have 'a' drink? He was having a laugh. Alcohol was one of the forbidden consumables. I suppose he thought he was being nice telling me I could have a drink. He didn't have a clue. I felt like misbehaving in epic proportions.

I went back to the bedroom and grabbed my phone. *Let's start early. Been months since I had even a sip of a drink. Start off in West Kirby, maybe grab an early dinner there?* I sent the text, had another thought and quickly composed another. *There's a new bar on the promenade. Fancy checking it out?*

Jimmy was still noodling around on his guitar, this was his main way of getting into 'deep think' mode. Must be some issues with work, I decided.

The phone beeped. *Can't wait. Meet at six o'clock at the Moby Dick?*

Yes. See you then. I wasn't sure if the evening could come quick enough. I needed to waste some time. I eyed the phone for a moment then grabbed it. I dialed and waited for an answer.

"Hello?"

"Mum, it's me."

"Kath, how are you? Chemo not got you too bad this time, I hope. Wasn't it yesterday you went?"

"I'm feeling good, Mum, really good. Do you think the farm still has strawberries? I feel like doing some picking. We could go together?"

"Are you certain you're up to that? I could come to you. I have some soup made, we could have lunch at yours."

"No, Mum. I want to go out. I really want some strawberries." I held my forehead with my free hand and tried to remain calm.

"What does Jimmy say?"

I sighed. I should have realized I'd be in for a big dose of mollycoddling. "I don't go asking Jimmy for permission. *I* decided I wanted strawberries. I thought you'd want to come with me."

"Don't get me wrong, dear. Of course I want to come."

I could hear the strain seeping into her words. I supposed she could hear the same with me. Maybe I shouldn't have called her.

"Kath, you still there?"

"I'm here, Mum."

"Why don't you come and get me? I'll tell you all about what your father's been up to." An attempt to dispel the bad feelings. Couldn't fault her for effort.

"Okay, Mum. See you in an hour." I hung up the phone thinking how the conversation was far harder work than I'd thought it would be. No one was used to me having energy these days, or being well enough to drive, or having the desire to go anywhere. If this machine did cure me, I realized it wasn't just me and Jimmy that would have to adjust. This was something that would send ripples out to all my family and friends.

I arrived outside Mum and Dad's little terrace house less than an hour later and beeped my horn. Time needed to go quickly and I was feeling impatient. I beeped again. Moments later my mother came out the door looking harassed.

"Hi Mum." I leaned over and gave her a brief cuddle as she sat in the passenger seat.

"You sure you're okay to drive? Didn't you have chemotherapy yesterday?" She buckled in, giving me a sideways confused expression.

"I am fine. Yes, I had chemo but I've sailed through this one." I grinned. "What I really, really want now is to pick several punnets of strawberries and sit in the car scoffing them all with you."

Mum opened her mouth to speak, but I interrupted.

That Elusive Cure

"I want a day when I'm not treated like a sick person." I glanced over at her. "Please, Mum. I just want to be treated as normal. Think back to two years ago, before I got ill." Clouds danced across the sky, and the sunny day threatened to turn to rain. I put the car in gear and pulled into the road.

Mum was silent for a moment then she said, "We'll eat them until we've got red juice dribbling down our chins."

She was smiling, perhaps a little guarded, but this was the best I could expect.

"So what's Dad up to while we're off fruit picking?"

Mum suddenly burst into tears. I pulled into a layby. "Mum, what's wrong?"

She struggled to speak for ages then finally managed to say, "I think your father has another woman."

"No…" I thought about Dad cheating on Mum. "No, I don't believe it."

Tissues had appeared from up her sleeve. She dabbed at her eyes and blew her nose. "There's this woman, a new woman at their boating club. Tess is her name. Tess and your father have gone off camping together."

"It's a club, Mum. There'll be a bunch of them. Why would you think Dad's bunking in with this other woman?"

"I just know. You don't live with a person for fifty years and not know when things have changed. Doesn't matter that others in the Old Codger's Club are there, I know what he's up to."

I didn't know what to say. Two years of being selfish and worrying about me and only me had destroyed my interpersonal skills. Rather than say the wrong thing, I sat quietly. I knew Dad had cheated on Mum when I was in college. Once with a secretary then a couple of years later with a neighbor who'd moved away. My understanding was that if he strayed again he'd be told to leave.

"He's out there now, somewhere in Wales, bedding down with that... with that *woman*." She spat the word out like it was venomous.

"I'm sure you're wrong, Mum. Do you want me to talk to him?"

She put a hand on my knee. "No, dear. You have enough to worry about. I'll deal with him." She blew her nose loudly. "I'm sorry. I've spoiled our afternoon out."

I leaned over and gave her a hug. "No, Mum. You haven't ruined a thing." And she hadn't. For once a tragedy wasn't about me. This felt normal, almost like a relief. A burden from my shoulders had gone. Maybe I could relearn how to be a member of the family, of the human race. I could stop being Cancer Kath and be simply me once again.

"Still want strawberries, or do you want me to take you home?"

Mum took a deep breath and put her tissue away in her sleeve. "I would very much like to pick some strawberries."

"Okay, then." I drove off towards the pick-your-own farm, having already decided that I was going to ignore her and speak to my father anyway, all the time wondering what on earth I was going to say to him.

FOURTEEN

Out With Janie

The taxi dropped me off at the Moby Dick in West Kirby just after six. Not so long ago the pub had been converted into a steakhouse, and was probably my current favorite restaurant. My resolve to have a wild mad night had been dampened by my mother's tears earlier. I'd almost cancelled with Janie, thinking that if I really had that much energy I should drive to where Dad was in Wales and catch him in the act or confront him or something. I wanted to think he was innocent, but Mum had been very convincing. And I hated to admit it, but didn't people say once a cheater always a cheater. Did that apply if there were decades between cheats?

I let out a long sigh as I climbed the steps into the pub. Shake it off, I thought. Tonight is about you and how damn brilliant your insides feel.

Janie was seated at the bar with another woman beside her. That kind of threw me, and for half a second I almost bolted. I saw tonight as a Janie and me only affair. I wasn't sure if I could cope with any additions. Somehow I made my legs work and walked up to them.

"Kath, hello!" Janie was in fine form. She had some brightly-colored cocktail in front of her, as did the other woman. She gave me a great big hug and sat back down.

"Hi…" I said, glancing nervously at the addition.

"This is Gill, my other half."

Gill waved and nodded towards her drink. "Would you like one?"

For half a second I didn't say anything. I looked from Janie with her short, brown, cancer-cut hair, her athletic figure and tomboyish clothes to Gill, a younger woman who I'd describe as slight with long light brown hair with a gentle wave. She was dressed in an almost romantic style, her shirt decorated with frilled edges and matched with a long flowing skirt. I remembered Janie saying her other half was called Gill, but I'd not actually made the connection of what that meant.

"I'd love one," I finally said and sat down.

My cocktail arrived quickly and I made a face at the sweetness, I wasn't used to so much sugar. But the alcohol soon warmed me up to the evening.

"How are the sessions going?" Janie didn't waste any time asking.

I glanced at Gill.

Janie laughed. "Don't worry. Gill knows all about what happened to me, don't you?"

Gill reached over and placed her hand over Janie's. "She didn't tell me at first. I guessed, there were too many changes happening too quickly. I cornered her and made her confess."

"That's actually a relief to know that. My other half, Jimmy, knows. He didn't notice a difference so much. You know what men are like. I'm not sure he'd notice if I came home with one of my arms missing." I chuckled. "He found out when he saw my car in the church car park."

"Oh shit, really?" Janie laughed.

"Yup. Caught me red-handed as I'd forgotten to lock the church door."

"So what did he do?" That was Gill.

"Found out where the machinery is, of course. Just can't help himself. Once he got over the weirdness of it all he wanted to know how it worked. He's been researching all kinds of cutting-edge technologies ever since."

Gill and Janie laughed.

"We ordered a mixed starter platter. Is that okay for you?" Janie said as the barman came over with an enormous plate piled high with all kinds of meat.

I sipped at my cocktail, surprised to find it almost gone already. I smiled at them. "Just what the doctor ordered," I said.

The evening went far too fast. We'd ended up at *Corks Out* a wine bar where you could get samples of different wines. You got a card which you topped up with money, then helped yourself to wine using the card to pay. Self-service – a quick road to complete drunkenness as I discovered. I got home earlier than I'd originally intended, threw up most of my wine and then crawled into bed. Jimmy was milling about, looking nervous. Probably because I was one day post chemo and really shouldn't have been leaving the house, let alone getting falling-down drunk. I smiled at the memory of Janie and Gill pushing me into the taxi and sending me home. I think I'd been making a fool of myself and dancing around singing loudly and badly. Then I passed out.

I woke up feeling less hung over than by rights I should have. Maybe my body was so out of practice that it had forgotten how. There were texts on my phone.

One from Janie: *Hope you're not feeling too awful today. Had a great time last night. We should do it again sometime. x*

And one from Cass: *Mum, need to talk to you. Can I come over today?*

I replied to Janie's: *Not feeling as bad as I should, lol. Thanks for the brilliant evening. Just what I needed. Lovely meeting Gill as well. She's as lovely as you. x*

Then Cass: *What's up love, something wrong? x*

I'll tell you when I get there. I'll come at two and bring cakes.

I glanced at the clock, it was nearly 11. If I was going to get my session in with the machine I was going to have to hurry. With a spring in my step, I went to the bathroom for a shower. Jimmy was nowhere to be found, but no matter. He was probably down the end of the garden doing his Saturday morning yoga exercises. There was a need growing in me, like an addiction. I needed to go to the machine, I *had* to be there. Didn't matter what got rearranged or missed out on, I would go there as soon as I'd washed and dressed.

Whistling a merry tune, I dug into the box of tampons for the key to the church. It wasn't there. Cold panic came over me. I dumped the box out on the floor in the bathroom. No key. I rifled through the drawer. No key. I ripped the drawer out and dumped that on the floor. No key. Shit, where was Jimmy? I climbed on the toilet seat and opened the bathroom window and peered down at the driveway. Jimmy's car was gone. Shit. Screw being clean. I ran back to my bedroom and dressed. What the hell did he think he was up to?

Staying just long enough to give my teeth a rough brush and drink a cup of orange juice, wincing at the combination of tart with the minty toothpaste, my tummy was giving me the first signs of upset from the night before. Or maybe it was sickness thinking what the hell was he doing, sneaking off to the church? Shit, shit, shit. I grabbed my keys and left, almost taking out the garden wall as I sped away.

I pulled into the tiny church car park, blocking Jimmy's car in. Leaping out I bolted for the church, hoping he hadn't locked the door, unsure of how I'd get in if he had. The door handle turned smoothly and I threw it open, the door bouncing off the wall. Jimmy was there, crouched down behind the pod. He jumped at the loud bang and I heard the tinkle of tools dropping.

"You're here…" he sounded nervous.

"Of course I'm bloody here. I'm supposed to have a session today, as you know. So, are you going to tell me what the hell is going on, Jimmy?" I slammed the door shut and marched up to him.

That Elusive Cure

"Nothing, I thought I'd have a look at the machinery, try and work it out." He stuttered his words. He was hiding something.

"Oh my God." I stopped. Jimmy had opened the panel of the pod. Tools were strewn all around him. There was an extension cord that led away behind some pews with a soldering iron and drill plugged in. He was sat on the parquet flooring, staring at the machinery and avoiding my glare. The first thing I noticed was the missing pipe. "You've broken it." The words came out as a whisper. My cure, my fix, my remission, he'd stolen them from me.

Tears came suddenly. I backed up, tripping over his tool bag and landing heavily on my backside. "You broke it!" I said again, unable to comprehend. I was almost fixed, almost cured. How could he? I wiped at the tears, a long moan coming from deep inside. "How could you do this to me?"

"It wasn't my fault, I wanted to have a go in the machine. I climbed in and before it could do anything there was a hissing noise from inside. I managed to get the back open and I was going to fix it."

"You broke it," I repeated.

"No, I didn't." He put a hand up to stop me shouting back. "It broke all by itself. I was trying to fix it. But as soon as I saw the insides I knew I had to try and figure out how it worked. If I could make more of them I could cure the world. We'd be billionaires, the world at our feet..."

"So you opened it up and the pipes came jumping out at you?" I levelled my gaze at him.

"No... I was getting a better look." He picked up the broken pipe. "And that's when this happened."

My hand came to rest on a book, I grabbed it and threw it at him. "I don't care about how it works or the rest of the fucking world. You've killed me, that's what you've done!" Great sobs took me over. I pulled my legs up and buried my head in my thighs. A hand tentatively touched my shoulder, and I shook him off. "Get away from me!" I screamed.

"I'll fix it, I promise."

"Empty fucking words, Jimmy. Couldn't you have waited until I was done? One more session, you hear me? One more bloody session and I'd have been fixed." I raised my head and wiped at the tears. "I wanted to live, don't you get it? How can you even begin to understand the machine? The technology you need to fix it probably doesn't even exist yet."

Jimmy pulled out his phone. "That's where you're wrong. The pod is based on nanotechnology. There's research being done on this in a lab in-"

"I don't care!" I knocked the phone from his hand. "All I wanted was to be cured. Be the miracle. And you've bollocksed it all up."

Jimmy gave me a wounded look and reached for his phone. "I wanted to give you a good life-"

"You just don't get it, do you, Jimmy. The machine *was* going to give me a good life. All I ever wanted was to live a bit longer with no pain and no more soul-destroying treatments." Anger had dried up my tears. Ignoring Jimmy, I got up and went to the machine and touched the side to open the lid. I kicked off my shoes and climbed in. The mattress was still doing its thing, but I didn't think that was mechanically driven. It was simply a new type of memory foam. Just in case he'd not broken anything critical, I hoped beyond hope and reached up to the panel above me.

Nothing happened. I tried again, placing my hand flat against the smooth metal. The lid didn't budge.

I rested my hands across my tummy and lay there quietly. The machine had bought me some time, that's what I needed to dwell on, not Jimmy's stupidity. I understood now why he hadn't argued so much about me going out for drinks. Why I didn't remember having issues with him when I stumbled in the door just after midnight and immediately made an offering to the porcelain gods. He'd found the key and already had plans for while I was out.

Jesus, stupid man. I massaged my liver, feeling the shape of it where my ribs ended. Just a couple of weeks ago I could make out the shape of the larger tumors under my skin. Now all I felt was smoothness. Maybe the doctors could do more for me now, give me treatments that weren't previously open to me. I kept my eyes closed, squeezing them until I saw a shower of silver lights behind my eyelids.

Janie was going to have to be told that my stupid other half broke this gift, this wonderful machine. She'd forever be the last person to have the miracle given to them. Tears welled up in my eyes again and I felt them trickle down the sides of my face. Stupid, stupid man.

"Kath, I'm sorry."

Jimmy was nearby. Probably watching me as I lay cocooned in the mattress. No chance he was getting the satisfaction of a response, of forgiveness. Not now, not any time soon.

"Kath, I really thought I knew what I was doing."

I squeezed my eyes even tighter. Shame ears couldn't shut as well.

"I researched and had schematics for primitive versions of this one. I really thought I was prepared. I had no idea it would break so easily."

I took a deep breath and keeping my eyes closed replied, "Can you fix it?"

There was silence for a moment. Then Jimmy said, "Some sort of gas came out. I don't know what it was. All I know is it was really bloody cold. I blocked up the hole before it could all escape. I was going to come back with a small bottle and try and capture some. There's a lab in Liverpool I can send it for testing. Once I know what it is I can recharge the system and fix the break."

"Jesus." My hands moved from my stomach to my forehead. I rubbed at the headache that was growing there. "So the real answer is, no you can't fix it."

"Kath, that's not fair. I'll fix the machine. I just need to know what I'm dealing with."

"Whatever." I had no more patience for him. "I've got to go. Cass is due at ours later. I need to calm down before she gets there and you're not helping."

I wished for a dose of that calm-down magic the machine gave me to reduce my heart rate. Finally, I opened my eyes and glared at the shiny metal panel in the lid above me. I willed the machine to work, to fix my tumors, to make me healthy again. Out of the corner of my eye I could see Jimmy sitting on the pew that had been pulled up close to the pod. He was staring at the floor and holding his head in his hands.

I climbed out of the pod and slipped my shoes back on. "Where's the key?" I asked as I picked up my handbag.

Jimmy pulled it out of his jeans pocket and handed it to me without a word, not even daring to look at me.

The key was warm in my hand, solid, somehow making everything more real. I fought tears back, blinking hard to clear my sight. "You'll need it to lock up. Give me the key when you get home." I handed it back and turned on my heel.

"Fix it," I ordered as I walked out the door.

FIFTEEN

Cass has News

The hangover was catching up on me. I *needed* my session in the machine. How long before that git of a man managed to fix the damage he'd done – would he ever be able to? I lay on the sofa, one arm across my face. This was not how things were supposed to happen. A big part of me wanted Jimmy to stay away and never come home. What a bloody idiot.

The doorbell went. What now?

Cass didn't wait for me to get to the door, she let herself in. "Mum, hello Mum? I'm here!"

I'd forgotten she was coming. "I'm in the living room, Cass," I called out. My tummy was a mess and now I wasn't sure if that was the chemo catching up with me or punishment for drinking too much or Jimmy's antics making me feel ill. What I needed was my anti-sickness pills, and probably sooner rather than later.

"Oh Mum, you look awful." Cass put down a carrier bag and came over to the sofa to give me a hug.

As soon as her hands touched me, the tears came. I grabbed onto her tightly as the tears grew to sobs.

"Mum, what's wrong?" Cass held me tighter as I cried for the loss of my miracle. I cried for the loss of my life and for the cruel snatching away of a future I'd long ago given up on. Over the last few days I'd allowed myself just the beginning of a dream that I might grow old with Jimmy. But I couldn't tell her that. I let the tears flow.

"Mum, tell me what's wrong." Cass pulled away and found a tissue for me.

I wiped my face and blew my nose. "Don't worry about me. I'm just feeling bad because I had chemo a couple of days ago." Chemo, the universal excuse for anything at any time.

"How'd that go? Last one for a while, right? You must be relieved." She rubbed my arm, her eyes glassy as she also fought with her emotions

Tears welled up again, and I dabbed my eyes with the tissue. "I guess so," I said.

"You need a good cup of tea. Stay there." Cass left me on the sofa to wallow in my misery. I heard her fill the kettle and wondered what I'd done to end up with such a wonderful daughter.

"Here." She was back with two mugs of steaming tea along with some plates. "I promised cake, and I never you let you down, do I?" Cass put the teas down and rummaged around in the carrier bag pulling out a small carrot cake. "I even got the organic one." She cut a couple of slices and handed me one. "It's good, isn't it? There's a bakery near me that's started to stock all kinds of organic things. I can get you bread, buns and cakes. Just let me know if you want anything and I'll bring it." She sat down on the sofa next to me.

I took a mouthful of the cake, my stomach doing a little roll. Somehow I gave her a smile and muttered, "Yum."

"Where's Dad?" Cass was halfway through her cake already. I'd managed two tiny bites.

"He's out looking for parts for something."

"What's he up to now? Has he got some new project up his sleeve?"

Despite her cheery demeanor, I almost burst into tears again.

"He's always got something new to fidget with, hasn't he?"

Cass nodded and put her empty plate on a side table. "Look Mum, I'm not going to beat around the bush. I've got some news."

Suddenly she looked nervous, fiddling with her fingers and avoiding eye contact. I took a deep breath. I wasn't sure how much more 'news' and other people's problems I could take.

"What's wrong?"

She blurted out, "Mum, I'm pregnant."

I almost dropped my plate. "You're what?"

"Pregnant, Mum." She glanced at me and then looked away quickly. I could see desperation in her eyes, a desperate need to be accepted.

"How… how far along?" I stuttered my words. I think I might have been going into shock.

"About ten weeks. We're not sure. We're waiting for the scan to confirm. It wasn't exactly planned, so we're not certain when I conceived."

I closed my eyes for a moment, trying to process the information. "Oh, Cass. You're so young."

"I'm the same age you were when you had me," she said, her tone defensive. "And don't go telling me it was different back then. If it was different, it was only in bad ways."

I put a hand on her knee and then leaned over to give her a hug. "Oh sweetie. Congratulations."

That was what she'd needed. It was her turn to cry, and for just a moment I realized what a couple of headcases we were as she sobbed on my shoulder. A smile came to my lips and suddenly I was giggling. This was a good thing, a new life, positive news for once.

"I'm going to be a granny!"

Cass pulled away and this time I handed *her* a tissue.

"You're going to be a mummy." I smiled at her and kissed her on the cheek. "You'll be wonderful."

"Thank you, Mum." The relief in her voice was almost palpable. "I love you, Mum."

"Love you too, sweetie." I waited as she sipped her tea and tried to compose herself. "What does Jack make of all this?"

Her eyes suddenly sparkled. "He's made up, Mum. He can't wait for the baby to be born. All he does is talk about plans for the future."

I nodded, her happiness infectious. A car pulled up outside, and I heard the front door open quietly. That was Jimmy, slinking in.

"Dad," Cass called out. "Dad, come in here." She glanced at me and flashed me a teary smile. "I've got some news for you."

"So, are you never going to talk to me again?" Jimmy was stretched out on the sofa eating popcorn.

I was pretending to watch the television, thinking over and over how I could have stopped Jimmy from being so stupid. I should have hidden the key better, or taken it with me, or left it with Sal for safekeeping. I knew there was no point in going over it again and again, but it was like my mind was a record that kept repeating the same damn chorus.

For now I didn't want to reply to Jimmy, but not saying anything would just prove his point, so I said, "Of course I'll talk to you."

Cass had gone a few hours earlier, happy to have approval for her pregnancy from us both. I thought about her as Jimmy crunched on his popcorn. It was going to be tough raising a baby, her and Jack were so young. But then isn't it always hard to raise a baby? Didn't really matter how old you were.

"If you're talking to me then answer me this. How long are you going to be cross with me?" He munched and crunched and then said, "I'm sorry, okay. I didn't mean to break it."

Jimmy didn't sound sorry and I knew I didn't sound forgiving so I kept my mouth shut. My insides were in a bit of a swirl. Chemo nausea seemed to be catching up to me without the healing power of the pod. How long before the tumors regrew? I guess, worst come to worst, the machine had given me time, something I'd have considered a precious gift a few weeks ago.

Suddenly I had an idea. I flipped open my phone and composed a text to Janie.

That Elusive Cure

Any chance you could send me the details of the man who gave you the key to the church?

I didn't have to wait long. My phone beeped.

Why do you want his details?

I thought about a way of asking her that would convince her to give up his name and number. I smiled as it came to me. I typed fast.

I want to say thank you to the man who gave us the machine. I was going to try and work my way through all the people who've received treatment with it.

She'd either bite or she wouldn't. But if we could find the first person, maybe he would know where it came from, and maybe even how to fix it. I swore under my breath at Jimmy once more. Why did he feel the need to tinker with everything?

Janie took a little longer to reply, but she came up trumps.

I was told the guy who started it all is called Rich Newland. I think he owns the church. The guy who gave me the key was a man called Dave. I'll text you his number.

For a brief moment I actually smiled. Of course, I could go through the property records in the council and find this Rich Newland that way. At the same time I should keep working backwards through the cured people. Make sure I came at the problem from all angles.

My phone beeped again and there was a landline number there. Janie was wonderful. I texted her my thanks, leaving far too many 'x's.

"Something's cheered you up." Jimmy was no longer watching the television. He'd turned my way, staring at me as I typed on my phone.

I tried to calm the giant grin on my face. "I may have a lead on the guy who put the machine in the church. Maybe he knows where it came from, and maybe he has an idea about fixing the damn thing."

Jimmy sat up. "Really?"

It was then that I noticed the lines of regret etched in Jimmy's face. If I had to guess, I'd say he'd aged five years in a day. I sighed. Now wasn't the time for a war. "Jimmy, will you promise me you won't fiddle in the machine any more, and that you will not break any more of it?"

"Does this mean you love me again?"

"Promise me, Jimmy."

"I promise not to break or tinker with the machine anymore, other than when I fix it, which I will."

I nodded. That was the best I could hope to get from him.

"Oh, you had post this morning. Did you see it?"

"No?" I stood up and started towards the hall. "Is it on the shelves?"

Jimmy grunted an affirmative. There it was, a brown envelope, the type only the hospital seemed to use. I ripped it open.

"It's for my scan," I said as I walked back into the living room. "It's on Tuesday, early."

"Which kind has the doc ordered?"

"It's for an MRI at Arrowe Park. Seven-fifty in the morning."

"Why are they always so early? They never give you a reasonable time slot, like four in the afternoon." Jimmy started crunching on his popcorn again, back to half watching the TV.

That Elusive Cure

I thought about how lucky I was to be getting so many scans with such a short wait. When I thought about the stories I'd heard from people in other parts of the country waiting weeks for a scan, I knew how fortunate I was. Early or late in the morning, I didn't care. This was going to be the proof of the machine. I'd get to see if it really was working and how far towards cured that last session had taken me.

Once again butterflies erupted in my tummy. What would the doctors do when they saw my lung was clear? Maybe the other one would be clear now as well. I couldn't help but smile to myself. At the same time I felt my emotions well up and threaten to bring tears. If my lungs were clear I knew that opened me up to all sorts of other treatments that had been denied to me for so long. Even if the machine never worked again, it may have put my health on a brand new path, one I thought closed forever.

I put the letter down and joined Jimmy on the sofa. I snuggled up against him, feeling safe as he wrapped an arm around me. I didn't really watch the television, but closed my eyes and dreamed of what the doc's reaction to my scan might be.

SIXTEEN

Going to Wales

"Wake up, Jimmy."

I gave him a gentle push and was rewarded with a soft snoring sound.

"Jimmy, wake up!"

I shoved harder this time, rocking him back and forth. Jimmy flopped onto his back, opened one eye and tried to make out the time on the clock.

"It's ten o'clock, a perfectly reasonable time to be getting up," I told him. "We're going to Wales."

"It's Sunday, are you insane?"

"Yup, and I'm taking you down with me. Now *move*."

Jimmy yawned, adjusted his pillows and sat up just a little. "Exactly why are we going to Wales?"

For a moment I thought about fudging the truth. But I didn't do well being covert with Jimmy. "Dad's sailing at Bala Lake. I want to go see him."

"Bala Lake…?"

"Yes, there's an issue I've got to sort out."

"An issue…?"

"Stop repeating what I'm saying, it's annoying."

That Elusive Cure

"Annoying?" Jimmy smirked and I ignored him.

"Mum thinks Dad's cheating on her with this woman who's joined the Old Codger's Club."

"Don't be so silly. He wouldn't cheat." Jimmy closed his eyes again.

I shoved him. "He's done it before. Ages ago, before we got together."

"You're kidding me?" He seemed to be paying attention now. "Your dad, cheating?" Jimmy frowned. "Even if he did screw around on your mother once upon a time, can't quite see it happening now."

"Apparently, she thinks he is. Anyway I want to go there and find out what's going on."

"You want to catch him in the act."

I hesitated. That wasn't what I wanted to do. Catching in the act was something I really didn't want to do. I wanted this to be a misunderstanding so I could go back to Mum and tell her everything was okay, and that I'd sorted it out. I realized that this was the type of thing I used to do all the time before I got ill: sorting problems out, fixing situations, and mending feelings. When exactly did cancer make me so selfish and self-centered? Sometime in the last two years I'd forgotten about everyone else.

"I want to find out what's going on, for Mum's sake. Besides, can you imagine my father cheating after so long?"

Jimmy didn't reply for a moment then shook his head. "Can't see it myself."

"Well, Mum's convinced and I won't be able to get Dad on his own at their house. I figured finding him at the lake would be a good start." I rolled out of bed. "I'm off for a shower. You're next."

Just before eleven we headed out the house. I knew Dad would be coming home today, and had my fingers crossed it was a good sailing day and he'd still be there. I thought about texting him that we were coming, but with a heavy heart I decided to keep that quiet until we got there. If he was up to something I needed to be able to catch him unawares.

Jimmy drove, I'd had a busy few days and slept for just over an hour. I woke up not long before we got to Bala, the town at the far end of the lake, with Jimmy giving me a not so gentle shove to wake me.

"Which campground is he at?" Jimmy had a map of Bala open on his iPad.

I yawned and tried to focus on the map. "Haven't the foggiest. Let's drive around the lake and look for Dad's car. There can't be that many campsites, right?"

Jimmy scratched at his stubble. "I dunno. There's a fair few listed here." He scrolled back and showed me a list of campsites.

"Just drive, okay? He'll be at one that's by the water so he can launch his dingy boat."

Jimmy drove down one side of the lake, stopping at three campsites along the way. We drove through a village at the other end of the lake and started up the other side. It was coming up on two o'clock and I was getting nervous that we'd come all this way for nothing. Time was getting on and we'd still not found him.

We pulled into the second campsite along the north side of the lake and my heart jumped. Dad's car!

That Elusive Cure

There were five small tents all in a row with five cars parked to one side along with a corresponding number of boat trailers tucked away. The Old Codger's Club, yay! We'd found them. After explaining to the owners of the site that I was the daughter of one of the campers, we were allowed to park-up for a couple of hours. Jimmy and I walked to the rocky shore and sat on an old tree trunk. The weather was coming from behind us, the wind whipping my hair into my face, a thin misty rain trying to turn into something wetter. Several boats were on the lake, all of them going great guns across the water. I spotted Dad's boat off to the left of us, as he tacked back up the lake. For an old guy, he sure was fit and able.

As I snuggled up to Jimmy, I thought about Mum and her fears. What if she was right? What if Dad was having some sort of senior-life crisis? Then it started, my first pity fest in days. Would I get to grow old with Jimmy? Would I have the luxury of going grey and wrinkly? Old couples made me so jealous, especially the ones that had obviously been together almost their entire lives, the way Jimmy and I would be if I was given the gift of life.

A year or so earlier an acquaintance, after learning of my illness, told me how she had a number of friends living with cancer and that until the end came, treatments gave them a reasonable quality of life. Problem was, she was past retirement age. The friends she spoke of were all in their sixties and seventies. I was a mere forty years old at the time. Her friends had seen their children grow up, get married, had the pleasure of seeing what kind of adults their children would become. They'd probably had grandchildren presented to them. They'd had their careers and made their mark on the world. They'd had a chance to travel or at least live a life with their husbands or wives. I wanted to stuff her words back into her mouth. I smiled and nodded and thought to myself how I'd be lucky if I made it to forty-five. Maybe I should have asked her what she was doing at forty-five and told her that was when I thought I'd be dying.

A tightening on my arm brought me back to the lake, the wind and the spitting rain. Jimmy was giving me a squeeze. We could see my dad on his boat.

"I'm sorry, Kath," Jimmy said and pulled me closer.

I focused, rubbed my eyes and hoped to see things differently, but nothing changed. Someone was sat with Dad, and that someone was a woman.

"I want to go." I stood up, too quickly and a rush of blood to my head made me stagger. The pebble beach crunched under my feet as I checked to see where our car was parked.

"You don't want to talk to him?" Jimmy sounded incredulous.

I shook my head as I glanced back at Dad's boat.

"After we came all this way?"

The wind picked up and I watched as Dad adjusted the sail and the boat suddenly took off. The woman in the boat gave a little shriek, the sound almost entirely snatched by a gust. I was sure I heard the shriek turn to laughter.

"I want to go," I said again, hearing my voice come out cold. How could Dad do that to my mother?

Nearly fifty years of marriage and this is how it ends. Dad sailing about with some middle-aged trollop on board. Didn't he learn his lesson the first two times he was caught? Mum had said three strikes and you're out. This was number three.

Jimmy remained sitting on the log. "I think you and your dad need to sort it out here and now."

"You're pissed off because I'm going to make you drive another hour and a half and you haven't had a break."

The clouds whipped by the tops of the hills that surrounded Bala Lake. Little white dots covered the gentle slopes leading out of the valley. It seemed if you had a green patch in Wales you put some sheep on it.

"Kath, that's not it. You won't be happy if you leave like that. You need to sort it out."

My face suddenly felt hot, tears were close. I turned my face towards the wind to try and cool my emotions. What was he doing cheating on Mum? Bastard! "No, we're going." My voice quivered. An urge to run came over me, to get far away before Jimmy and my father saw how upset I was. Stupid cancer got into everything. It was like a black mold that slowly choked the life out of everything around a person. I should have seen this coming, I should have been paying attention. So many things were going unnoticed by me. Cass was pregnant for God's sake. How did I not see that one coming?

Jimmy remained on the log and his lack of movement was beginning to really piss me off. He stared out into the lake and said, "He's seen you."

I saw Dad now, waving from the boat and using the wind to shoot him towards the shore. He'd be on dry land before I even reached the car at the rate his boat was going. If I wasn't so cross, so upset, so confused by what I'd seen I might have been impressed.

"Kath!" Dad shouted to me, a big smile on his face. So brazen, that woman sitting beside him. From the angle I had it looked like one of her hands was on his leg. Jesus! Did he think I couldn't see her or that I wouldn't notice her once he was on the shore?

Dad's boat got as close to the beach as he was going to allow it. He tossed a rope to Jimmy who was finally on his feet.

"Hold her steady, would you?"

Jimmy knew the drill and kept a firm grip of the rope as Dad climbed out of the boat and into the water, his waders keeping him dry. Between the two of them they got the boat on the pebbles and the woman climbed out. She made a beeline for me, a wide smile on her face.

I looked left, then right, searching for an escape route. All I could think is that this moment would forever be seared on my brain as the moment I met the woman who split up my parents. She'd not said a word and I already hated her. I backed up the bank and onto the grassy verge.

"Kath? Hello." The woman came at me, a hand extended in greeting. Before I had a chance to escape she had one of my hands, not to shake but to grasp with her own warm hands. "I'm Margret." She spoke with an educated accent and I imagined her coming from a wealthy family.

"Hi…"

That Elusive Cure

Dad and Jimmy had dealt with the boat and both were now heading our way. Jimmy was chatting with my father his hands skittering around as he spoke, a sure sign he was excited about something.

"Your father has told me so much about you. I'm sorry to hear about your health problems."

God was she smooth. How dare she, this home wrecker, how dare she talk to me like this.

"Kath," Jimmy said as he and Dad joined us. "It's not what you think." His eyes were gleaming.

"Hi sweetheart." Dad came up and placed a kiss on my cheek, his beard tickling my skin. "To what do I owe the honor of you hunting me down in Wales?"

I knew Dad must already know why I was here, he and Jimmy had spoken. I shrugged and looked to Jimmy for help. But all Jimmy did was put an arm around me and grin stupidly at Margret.

"You'll never guess what I've been up to." Dad smirked, glancing at Margret.

I was so confused, how could he think I would be pleased? My face was going hot again, despite the wind and the misting rain. No matter what, I wasn't going to let myself cry in front of this woman.

I shook my head, not trusting myself to speak.

"Margret here," he linked arms with her and gave her a gentle squeeze, "is helping me plan for your mother's and my fiftieth wedding anniversary."

The surprise hit me hard. Despite my best efforts tears were suddenly falling. He wasn't cheating, he was planning an event?

"Hey what's wrong?" Dad wrapped me up in his arms, and I was ten again, crying over the death of our cat, Jerry. Dad felt as big and strong and as comforting as he ever had.

"I thought… I thought…"

He cut me off. "Shush, don't worry. We'll talk about it later."

Jimmy must have had a damn quick chat with him as they worked on the boat.

But it should have been *me*. It should have been me that he came to for help, not this stranger. I was his family, he should have come to *me*. And I knew why he hadn't. I was the cancer daughter, the sickly woman who shouldn't be bothered. It would tire me or stress me, and how do you time meetings for secret events when your accomplice is sick with chemo or can only think about the latest upcoming scan? Here it was, one more facet of my life, stolen by this stupid disease. I hated it, hated every aspect of this sickness. How it slowly took away my very person. I'd be dead long before cancer stopped my heart.

I dragged my sleeve across my face to dry my tears, feeling like a petulant child, and tried to get my emotions under control.

Dad let me go and nodded at the small café. "Come on. I'll treat us to a tea and tell you all the plans."

SEVENTEEN

Finding Mr. Newland

I woke up and didn't move for a long time. Yesterday's turn of events still had me in a state of shock. My phone beeped and I grabbed it from the bedside cabinet. Oh, God. It was Janie.

How did your last session go? When do you have a scan? That's the proof of the pudding! :) Are you excited? xxx

Damn her and her attentiveness. How on earth was I going to fool her into thinking I was already cured? Shit.

Jimmy was in his study banging away on his keyboard and whistling tunelessly along to whatever music was coming through his headphones. It occurred to me that I didn't know Jimmy's plan to fix the pod. I put the phone down and chose to ignore the message for now. Maybe Jimmy would fix the machine and I could text her screams and shouts about how I was cured. Maybe pigs would fly.

"Oi, Jimmy." Feeling lazy, or maybe chemo tiredness, I wasn't sure, but I didn't feel like going to him. "Jimmy!" I shouted.

"What?"

"Come here, I want to talk to you."

I heard a sigh, and then a clunk as the headphones landed on the desk.

"What? Some of us are trying to work, you know."

I smiled, this was his daily disclaimer. My guess was he was scanning the *Daily Mail* headlines. He came into the room, went around the bed and opened the curtains a little. The sun came in, making me blink as Jimmy sat against the window sill.

"What's going on with the machine?"

"What do you mean?"

I rolled my eyes. "Your plan, dummy. To mend it."

"Well, I took a sample of the gas and sent it off to that lab I told you about. It went in the morning post."

"You've sent it off?" Surprised, I glanced at the clock. It wasn't even ten o'clock. That was dedication, even for Jimmy.

He nodded. "I found a research lab where this Dr. Handler is experimenting with nanotechnology. We've been chatting via email, and he agreed to test the gas."

"How much did you tell him?" Visions of a gang of white-coated scientists breaking into the church and stealing the pod made me tense up.

Jimmy must have noticed and said, "Don't worry, he only has a few details. He certainly doesn't know about the pod, and he doesn't know about the church."

"Then how did you explain the gas?"

"Ah-ha!" Jimmy beamed a wide smile at me. "I told him I was doing my own experimentation and needed a better lab to test what I'd managed to produce. He was so curious about what a 'civilian' might be able to come up with that I didn't even have to ask. Dr. Handler told me to courier over the sample. So I did."

He gave me a Cheshire Cat grin. He did realize that if it wasn't for him he wouldn't have any need to be pulling the wool over that poor scientist's eyes? I'd be fixed and ready to live to an old age.

"Well, I've got my own research to do." I said. "Who knows, maybe I'll be able to get some information to help you."

Jimmy cocked his head. "What are you up to?"

"Let me do my research and I'll let you know." I rolled out of bed. "Now, back to your study. Some of us have work to do, you know."

Was this forgiveness? Jimmy certainly took it that way, giving my backside a gentle slap as he left the room. Did I think it was forgiveness? No, not really. More like forced acceptance. All the anger in the world wasn't going to fix that pod.

I shrugged on my dressing gown and made my way downstairs. First things first, I filled the kettle and set it to boil. Then I got my laptop out and opened it up. On the Google page I typed in: *find out who owns a house*. The results came up. Of course, Land Registry. I clicked the link and read the page. £3 to find out who owned a property. I opened up a new page and pulled up a map of Birkenhead. I found the road the church was on and then Googled that for more information. I was rewarded with the street number and a post code. Back on the Land Registry site, I plugged in the info, paid my £3 and waited for the email with the information.

Amazing, just a minute later and I had it. My heart beat surprisingly quickly as I clicked the link and opened a webpage. A basic white form told me the on the third line that the owner was Richard Neil Newland and listed his address.

This was too easy, I thought as I jotted the information down on a piece of paper. Richard Newland lived in Calday, according to this, but the purchase had been made in 2002. Would he still be there eleven years later? I got out the phone book but couldn't find a listing. That didn't mean anything. It might simply mean he was ex-directory. Calday was just a few villages away from where I lived, no reason why I couldn't go to his house. But what if he turned me away or got me arrested? Worse, what if he demanded I hand the key back? Hardly anyone knew about the pod; what if he might think I was some sort of secret agent trying to steal the device?

Now I was I was getting paranoid. I managed to laugh at myself, but I knew I had to be cautious. Sending a letter might take a week to get an answer, but if I could make contact in the right way, it would be worth the wait.

Feeling rather like a stalker, I composed a letter to Mr. Newland. I crumpled it up and wrote another. That one ended up in the bin as well. What could I say that didn't make me sound odd? Odd would not get me an audience with him. Needing some time to think, I had a long shower and got dressed leisurely, mulling over words and phrases. I settled for this:

That Elusive Cure

Dear Mr. Newland,

I hope you don't mind me writing to you. I am very lucky to have possession of the key to your church. I am so grateful of your generous gift of the machine, and hope to be cancer-free in the near future.

My curiosity about the machine is tremendous, and I was wondering if you would be willing to tell me the history of how you came across it? All information will of course be treated as confidential.

I hope to hear from you soon.
Warm regards,
Kath Wyatt

With my contact details listed, giving him a choice of email, text, phone or letter, I figured I might have a shot of a reply. I sealed up my letter, stuck on a stamp and before I lost my nerve walked it down to the post box.

Now to deal with Mum. I checked my watch, Dad would have left for the boat club by now. I had about two hours to have my chat. Finding the address for Mr. Newland had buoyed me. I felt lucky, like I should be buying lottery tickets kind of lucky. Mum was going to be a doddle. All I had to do was explain about Margret, give Mum a cuddle as she cried with relief, then leave as Dad got home so they could have an evening of making up. Easy-peasy.

I walked home from the post box whistling, the sun on my face, a warm breeze blowing through my hair. There was an anniversary to plan, a mother to reassure, a baby to look forward to, and a scan to amaze the doctors with. I might not be cured yet, but life was good.

EIGHTEEN

Mum is Leaving

"Mum, it's me!" I called out as I closed her front door behind me. A noise came from upstairs. I slipped off my shoes and went upstairs to join her.

"What are you doing here?" Mum said. She was in her bedroom, her clothes spread out all over the bed and two suitcases open on the floor. "You should leave."

"Mum, what the hell is going on?" I didn't have to ask, it was blindingly obvious.

"I'll not stand for him having some floozy. I'm leaving." Her cheeks were flushed with anger.

I surveyed the mess. "Where are you going to go?"

Mum threw a handful of underwear in one of the suitcases. "It's already sorted. I'm going to your Auntie Pauline's."

"Stop, please." I grabbed her arm and forced her to sit on the bed.

She pushed the shirts out of the way and gave me a sour look.

"Mum, Margret isn't after Dad. Nothing's going on."

That Elusive Cure

For a moment I thought she was going to slap me. Then in a very low voice she said, "You've met this woman? Behind my back?" Mum choked back a sob. "How dare you."

I felt like a traitor. "Honestly Mum, it's not what you think. She's with Dave," I said and readied myself to tell the story the four of us had concocted at the lake.

"Salty Dave?" She shook her head. "I don't believe it. No one would want to be with that smelly old man. I should have known you'd take your father's side." She got up and started to pile trousers on top of the underwear.

"Mum, you've got to stop." I grabbed at her again, but she slipped from my grasp and swung. She'd grabbed a hairbrush and before I could see what was coming at me, clocked me on the chin. "Jesus, Mum. What the hell?"

"Get out of my house." She pointed at the door, her lips pursed into a thin line.

"Look, you're right. I wasn't telling you the truth."

Mum's hand dropped a bit, but her expression darkened. "What a surprise. Tell me then. Admit it. He's been cheating."

How had Dad not noticed things had got so bad?

"Mum, he's planning a surprise party for your 50th wedding anniversary."

For a moment, she seemed frozen to the spot, the color draining from her face. "Whaaa," she managed to say, then collapsed onto the edge of the bed.

"You know Dad, he's about as useful as a wet rag planning these things, so when Margret joined the Old Codger's Club he asked her to help."

"I – I – I found texts on his phone. For meet-ups."

"Yes," I said and took her hands.

"And they kept mentioning the date of our anniversary. I thought he'd forgotten the date and how ironic it was that he planned to leave me on that day."

I shook my head and passed her a tissue as the tears began to fall.

"I wasn't going to let him think he was getting one over me. That's why I decided to leave." She was really crying now. "But the texts I found, they make sense now."

"Oh Mum." I sat next to her and we cuddled, her shaking with sobs and me not much better.

Suddenly, Mum pulled back. "Your father can't know." She glanced about the room. "And you can't tell him I know about the party."

"I'll help you put the clothes back."

She touched my chin gently, tears welling up in her eyes as I winced. "I'm so sorry about hitting you. I don't know what came over me." Mum shook her head.

"I understand, Mum. At least I know you still love Dad," I said, smiling.

"You are telling the truth? He's not cheating, he's planning a party?"

"Yes Mum. I wouldn't cover up something like that. Ever."

Mum nodded, and we hugged briefly. I stepped back and surveyed the room. In her haste, Mum had pulled shirts from their hangers and tossed them onto the floor, jackets and jumpers half-hung off the bed in messy piles. Looked like she'd not started on the shoes yet. According to my watch, Dad would be at the boat yard for at least another hour. We had plenty of time to sort out the mess and for me to get Mum downstairs and feed her sweet tea to calm her down before he got back. Mascara trails ran down her cheeks, she'd have to give her face a wash as well.

My phone beeped and for a second I ignored it. There's something about phones and their insistent sounds. I just can't resist. Hoping it wouldn't be Janie asking about me being cured I glanced at the screen to see Jimmy's name.

"What's he want?" I said more to myself than Mum and clicked on the message.

He's coming. Only two words, but they gave me an unpleasant shiver.

Who's coming? I replied and went back to helping Mum.

The reply came almost instantly. *The scientist. He's showing up at ours in an hour.*

"Shit, that idiot." I slammed the phone down on the bed. There must have been something fantastic in the sample. Some new thing the scientist had never seen. Now he knew our home address. How long before Jimmy was seduced into showing him the church?

"What's wrong?"

Mum's short hair was uncharacteristically ruffled. I stared, noticing how the white overwhelmed her once blonde coloring. A few weeks ago I might have had a surge of jealousy, getting old seemed such an impossible dream. Now... well, I had a chance. Old age was within my grasp so long as my bumbling other half didn't allow the machine to get spirited away from us. She noticed my staring and smoothed her hair.

"It's Jimmy. He's up to stupid stuff again."

Mum hung up a shirt. "What's he up to this time?"

I tried to think of something, some story that she would believe, but I couldn't lie very well to my mother. I sat heavily on the edge of the bed. "It's a long story." I glanced at the clock. "I've got just over half an hour before I've got to be home. Jimmy's about to mess it all up and I've got to stop him."

Mum raised her wrinkled forehead in curiosity and eyed the last items scattered around the room. "Mess what up?"

"A cure."

Mum boggled at me. "Are you serious?"

I nodded, rubbing the material of a silk scarf between my fingers and avoiding eye contact.

"A real cure?" She took a step towards me.

"To be honest we don't know for sure yet. My scan is tomorrow."

"So this is something the doctors did? A new treatment?" She'd abandoned the last of the clothes.

"No..." How could I explain? As all good stories had to be told, I decided, at the beginning. "It's complicated."

Mum picked up a few pairs of trousers. "Are you going to tell me about it?"

I nodded and took a deep breath. "It all started a few weeks ago when I met this woman named Janie up at Clatterbridge."

NINETEEN

Meeting the Scientist

I raced home, wondering if I'd beat this scientist of Jimmy's to the house. Too much was going on all at once, and my head felt like it was filled with static.

Mum had been dumfounded by the story I told her. I left her sitting on the edge of her bed, the last of the clothes put away, but she had this look of disbelief that made me think she didn't trust what I was saying at first. Then she'd reached out to hold my hand, wrapping her fingers tight around mine and I realized what I was seeing wasn't disbelief, but guarded hope. Guess I recognized that feeling in myself.

I got onto the motorway and put my foot down. Who knows what Jimmy would tell this man, this stranger? I had to get there and direct the conversation, protect the secrets of the machine. Ten minutes later and I pulled up to my house. A beat up old Fiesta was parked half on the pavement. I came to a stop on the driveway and took a second look at the rust-spotted red car. This was not the type of car I expected to see a scientist driving.

"Jimmy?" I said as I walked in the door, and went straight into the living room.

A skinny young man dressed in an old concert t-shirt and faded jeans sat opposite Jimmy. He stood as soon as he saw me and extended a hand. "Dr. Handler." He cleared his throat, averting his eyes as if he was nervous. "Bob, my name's Bob."

I took his hand and shook. His palm was damp, his hand bony. "I'm Kath."

I sat down in my chair, glancing at Jimmy as I did so. He smiled, looking far too relaxed for my liking. Over-confident. That always meant trouble with Jimmy.

"So, what has Jimmy told you?"

"Oh, not much. I only just got here." Bob was talking to my shoulder. I decided maybe he had Asperger's.

I dipped my head to catch his eye. "You looked at the contents of the vial?"

Jimmy threw me a glare. Perhaps he thought I was stealing his thunder, but did he really think I was going to allow him free-rein with this conversation?

"Oh yes." Bob gave me a brief smile then glanced at Jimmy before staring at the wall. "I had to come and see you. I've been working on nanotechnology for the last ten years, and the sample you sent was years ahead of anything I've discovered. Where did you get the sample from?"

I tried to speak, but Jimmy got there first. "That's confidential." Jimmy stretched back on the sofa and clasped his hands behind his head. "I have this client. I'm bound by confidentiality. You know."

That Elusive Cure

What a load of poppycock. No way this kid scientist would fall for that. But I watched as Bob nodded vigorously.

"Of course. Confidential." He wrung his hands. "Why did you send me the sample then?"

Jimmy sat forward. "I need to know if you can make more."

For a few seconds, Bob didn't say anything. He glanced at me, then at Jimmy. "This is way beyond anything I have created."

My heart sank. The pod *must* have come from the future. Maybe the technology to replicate the little nano bits simply didn't exist yet. Tears sprang from nowhere. That was it, dream over. Jimmy sank into the sofa, the cocky smile vanishing.

"But that's not to say I can't." Bob took a notebook out of his back pocket. "I've made some quick calculations. I think with time I could replicate the particle. The main problem is..." he licked a finger and flipped through the pages, "there's this element of the particle that I need to figure out, it's completely new to me. The biometrics are all wrong, and there seems to be an intelligence in the individual particles with a nanoelectronic biosensor I've not come across. I've been using liposomes as a transport mechanism, but in the sample they seem to work differently. Even if I can't replicate them, these seem advanced enough that if I introduce the right medium, I might be able to get them to self-replicate. I just need to beware the grey goo."

He chuckled at this last statement, like I should understand what was clearly an inside 'scientist' joke. I stared at him, not having understood much of anything he said, but impressed that Bob really did seem to have a clue.

"Do you have a timescale?" Jimmy asked. He looked as perplexed as I felt.

Bob flipped through a couple more pages, scanning the notes there. "One year. Maybe two... probably two."

Two years? Could I last that long? Jesus to be so close to being fixed and then have Jimmy break my only hope. I narrowed my eyes and waited until Jimmy glanced my way so I could make my disappointment known.

"I'll have to pull late shifts, I can't be seen working on this. Can't let Phil see this." Bob was mumbling, not really speaking to us. Then louder he said, "Do you know what this means?"

I shook my head as Bob made eye contact for a second.

"This is Nobel Prize winning stuff. This could change the world." Bob was back leafing through his notebook. "What's it do?"

"I'm sorry, what do you mean?"

"The particle? What is its purpose?"

"You need to know that?"

Bob nodded. "It'll be hard to make more and know they're working if I'm not sure what they are supposed to do. From my brief time with it under the microscope today I know it's for medical purposes, but for what?" He paused for a second and said flippantly, "Is someone trying to cure cancer?"

Jimmy and I exchanged glances. How much should we tell him? That it cured people? Just how much we didn't even know ourselves. Jimmy turned my way, leaving it up to me to say what I wanted.

"I – I – uh…" I stumbled over words. "Look, it's a top secret thing. It fixes people."

Jimmy gave me a pained look, he obviously thought I'd told too much. But how was Bob supposed to make more if he didn't know what it did?

"Fixes what?"

"Um," I glanced at Jimmy. "Everything. I think. To be honest we're not sure how many things it cures."

Bob was almost jiggling in his seat. "Wow. Just, wow." He grinned at both of us. "Thank you for trusting me. This is bigger than big." He made some notes on the pad, scribbling away manically for a couple of minutes.

Jimmy got up and came over to me, perching on the arm of the chair and putting an arm around me. I tensed and tried to push him away.

"Is there no way you could tell me where this sample came from?"

Jimmy shook his head. "Sorry."

"It's amazing, you know. A perfect little particle." Bob gazed off into the distance then turned our way. "I hope you don't find it too odd that I had to come and meet you, I had to try and see where you found the sample."

I shrugged. "Maybe another time."

Bob stood, hitching up his jeans before hesitantly offering his hand again. "I'd better go. Long ride back to the Midlands. Bessie doesn't like driving at night."

"Bessie?" I couldn't help but ask.

Bob pointed out the window. "My car. She's been with me since I was a student. You could say she's my good luck charm."

I looked curiously at Bob, deciding my first assessment of him wasn't right. Maybe I could warm to this man. He shoved his hand into mine and we shook, this time a warm, dry palm touching my own.

Jimmy and I saw him off, watching Bessie cough out black smoke as she lurched up the street.

"He seemed to know what he was talking about." There was tension in the air between us, and I know it was all my doing. I took a deep breath and said, "I guess you picked the right guy for the job. But two years…"

"Think you can last that long?" Jimmy was staring after the coughing Fiesta, not daring to turn his face to mine.

"Scan's tomorrow. I guess we'll find out soon."

Jimmy put an arm around me and pulled me close. I refused to hug him back and stood awkwardly against him, arms at my sides. Two years, I honestly didn't think I'd have that long.

I heard him whisper, "I'm so sorry," into my hair. The abyss of an early death was catching up with me again, and I was in no mood to let Jimmy think he'd be forgiven. I shrugged him off and went back inside.

TWENTY

The Scan

Freddie Mercury belted out the words to *Somebody to Love* as I settled into the MRI scanner. The earphones were snug on my ears and as always, I'd brought along my *Best of British* CD. The nurses had admitted to singing along to the songs before, and it had become a favorite of mine when I had to go in the machine.

My fingers twitched around the alarm bell and as the nurses inched the cot bed back and forth, searching for the ideal position to put me in, I fretted that the line into my arm would snag on something. But I needn't have worried. One of the nurses muted my music and asked if I was okay.

"Yup, fine here," I said. I knew the drill. I'd had far too many of these.

The machine started up, clanging and banging over Freddie's smooth vocals. I never opened my eyes in the scanner; I'd been warned about how claustrophobic the MRI was before my very first one. So I did what I always did. As Freddie faded out and Mick took over with *Brown Sugar*, I concentrated on the pattern of the bangs, swooshes, zaps and shuck-shucks of the machine and slowly fell asleep.

My sleep was thin and vague dreams tried to materialize. Cured. Remission. A doctor telling me I was a miracle. Me jumping around screaming and shouting as Jimmy beamed with delight. A bright sunny day, a new beginning.

I woke up feeling the weight of the results on me already. I had an appointment for Thursday with my oncologist, and I had an odd feeling of the date being both too soon and too far away at the same time. Nerves fluttered up in my belly as the nurses reversed the cot bed out of the MRI scanner. As usual one of them was already talking to me even though I still had the earphones on.

"I can't hear you," I said and gave her a smile. The straps of the cot bed still held my arms down, so I waited for the nurse to pull them off.

She removed the earphones and put them away. "Sorry love. I'm just going to remove the restraints. She ripped the Velcro straps apart and took away the various layers of padding while I yawned and tried to wake myself up. Jimmy was waiting for me in the waiting area, a pre-celebration breakfast at our favorite pancake place planned. But pre-celebration wasn't the right term, that was ripe for jinxing. It was an end of chemo reward. I'd tell Jimmy when I saw him. No point mucking everything up now.

"I'm just going to take the cannula out now, please stay lying down."

I watched as she pulled the line out of my arm and pressed a wad of gauze on the hole. Without needing to be asked, I took over pressing it down while she got the tape. The nurse helped me sit up and I went through to the changing room to get back into my clothes. I held my arm up above my head, pressing on the padding in an attempt to stop any bruising. This usually worked, or at least limited the bruising I'd get. I sat down on the bench, staring at my pile of folded clothing and wondering what I'd do if the scan didn't show what I wanted it to. For the first time in a while I doubted the ability of the pod. Despite the energy I felt, the way chemo hadn't turned me into a energyless zombie, that I hadn't spent days crouched over the loo emptying my guts out, that drizzle didn't feel like acid on my skin from the nerve damage, I still couldn't entirely give myself in to thinking the pod had been fixing me before Jimmy ballsed it up.

I got dressed slowly, wondering how on earth I was going to get through the next two days.

A rap on the door made me jump. "Are you okay in there?"

"Yes, I'm fine. Just moving slowly."

"Okay, love. Let me know before you go."

"Will do." I just wanted to be alone with my thoughts. Have my fears and hopes mixing in my mind without distraction. I put my shoes on quickly, and left, giving a wave to the nurse as requested and going out to find Jimmy slouched in a seat and playing about on his phone.

"Get this."

He flashed his phone past my eyes, like he expected me to read what was there in the two seconds he paused.

"Our mate Bob has been working all night. He's sent me an update. It seems he loves this little particle of ours. He's been breaking it down under the microscope and digging up its secrets."

Jimmy looked pleased with himself. I sighed. Who knows, maybe this was how things were supposed to be, fate as it were. Jimmy breaks the machine. Bob figures out the machine. Bob and Jimmy make more machines and no one need be ill again. Could it fix old people? Make their organs like new again? Could the pod make a person live forever? I got a flash of an overcrowded world. Maybe it should be kept secret and safe.

We arrived at *Pancakes etc.* in Moreton and sat at a table by the window. Neither of us talked much as Jimmy ate his usual maple syrup pancakes while I had the banana topping. The weight of the scan had silenced us both. Not able to eat any more, I sipped my tea and stared at the people passing by on the street.

"Do you really think it's worked on me?"

Jimmy didn't reply. He just shrugged and pushed his empty plate back a little, patting his stomach while he did so. "It's hard to hope, isn't it?" He stretched out and sipped at his coffee. "You seem so well. That can't be faked."

"There's been a ton of research on the effect of placebos. You know as well as I do that me being so well could just be in my mind."

Jimmy joined me in people watching. I saw a fat woman go by pushing a pram with a squalling child. Why was it that I got ill when I tried to take good care of myself and people who ate rubbish and never exercised stayed healthy? I knew I was being a bitch, but it didn't stop the thoughts from coming. I had no right getting ill. I had plans to live to 101. I was going to write an essay about how the world had changed in my time, typed up on a keyboard and screen that I'd unroll and put wherever I felt like typing. I'd talk to walls with huge screens saying hello to my grandchildren, pioneers settling in on Mars. I'd tend my hydroponics garden, the type everyone had, growing the veg I loved most. And when I felt ready, that I'd said all I needed to, done all things I wanted to, loved to the limits of my ability, I could choose the time of my death, say goodbye in a big celebration and die with a smile.

TWENTY-ONE

Meeting Sally

I tried to sleep in on Wednesday, hoping to sleep right through to Thursday and the appointment. But of course, that wasn't possible. I lay there, picking at my nails, the nerves mounting inside me. What would they find? Fewer tumors, and I'd leave as they called me a miracle? Or no change, and the inevitable discussion about what they'd do now the chemo isn't working anymore.

My fingers hurt. I did this before every scan appointment. Pick, pick, pick. It was a compulsion that had graduated to part of the process of waiting to see my oncologist. Dr. Noble would come in as his happy dappy normal self, or he'd be serious and somber, and that was when we had to worry.

The phone ringing drew me out of circular thoughts. Jimmy was hard at work, earphones on, music at high volume no doubt. I threw off the covers and ran for the phone.

"Hello?"

"Hello Kath, it's just me, your old dad."

"Hi-ya. What can I do for you?" I sat on the floor, twisting the handset away from my mouth as I yawned.

"I wanted to thank you for talking with your mother." His voice sounded muffled. I wondered where she was and whether he realized that right now he was very unlikely to get anything over on my mother. "She's been much happier since you two had your talk. I take it she fell for the story?"

"Oh yes," I lied. "Hook line and sinker. You're in the clear now."

"Excellent. Lots of planning to do." He paused for a moment and I wondered if Mum was nearby. "I'd like it if you helped. If you're up to it, that is?"

My first thought was that Jimmy had set this up, and I felt a little ruffled. People shouldn't have to be told to include me. "I'd love to help," I said before he thought my hesitation was a negative thing. I told myself that it didn't matter why he'd asked. Just that he had.

"Look, your mother's coming. I'll call you again with a meet-up time."

I suppressed a laugh, Dad would have made a terrible spy. "Okay, Dad."

"Speak soon." He went to put down the receiver and I heard muffled excuses about a wrong number.

I put the handset down and thought about how I was going to pass the day. How long had it been since I last saw Sally? Guilt washed over me, what if she was struggling? I'd been so wrapped up in me and my issues, I'd forgotten about her. Didn't school holidays start soon? She'd need my support. No, that wasn't the right way around. It was the kids who would need my help in supporting their mother.

The pod floated into my mind like an apparition. Tomorrow I'd know if it really did fix me, or at least had gone most of the way towards fixing me. If it had worked, if the machine actually mended people, what was the extent of its ability? Could it balance the chemicals in Sally's brain, make her happy and stay that way? Give the kids a turn to soften the bad memories? What else could the pod do? More than ever I wanted that machine fixed.

Given her recent mental health, I decided not to let her know I was on the way. I got ready, gave Jimmy a wave goodbye and drove off, thinking of scientist Bob and his teenager's clothing and rust bucket car. Hopefully he was up to his ears in figuring out the secrets of the particles. Two years was so far away. Jimmy said it might be even longer and to prepare myself for a long wait. I pulled up to Sally's thinking I wasn't prepared for a wait, and that skinny little scientist had better get a move on.

I rang the doorbell. Would she be in a state? Would she be willing to have a visitor? Was she recovering from this latest downer? I tapped my foot and checked my watch. The time was coming up on one o'clock. I'd thought maybe she'd let me take her out for lunch.

"Hello, Sally?" I banged on the door and rang the doorbell a couple more times. "It's me, Kath."

Cupping my hands I tried to peer through the dappled glass in the door. Something moved by the kitchen.

"Sally, are you okay?" I shouted out and banged frantically.

The shape shifted and took a step towards the door.

"Sally, I can see you're there. You're worrying me. Please come answer the door." I thought about threatening her with getting the police or fire brigade to bash open her door. She'd hate me for it, but better that than the million bad things I could suddenly see happening.

"Sally, come on! Please open the door!"

Through the glass, shadows and shapes grew. Thank God, she was going to let me in. The door opened and instead of the soft features of Sally I was faced with Wendy, her sister.

"She's not here." Wendy barred my way in.

"Well, where is she? I want to see her."

I took a step forwards with a view to going inside, but Wendy stepped onto the threshold and pulled the door to behind her. I always thought Wendy was a hard-looking woman. She was a fair bit older than Sally with steely grey hair and not much resemblance to her sister other than both being far too slim.

Wendy crossed bony arms across her chest and glared at me. "You can't. She's in the hospital."

"You what?" My mouth gaped. "You've had her sectioned?" I nearly slapped her smug face. "How could you do that to her, your own sister?"

"It was for her own good. She was psychotic. Seeing that dead husband of hers… and the state of the house was horrendous. It's all I've done since I got here, clean and clean."

"I came by last week, she was improving." I tried to catch a look inside the house. "You sure she's not here?"

"She went off two days ago."

"Sally?" I shouted. "Sally, are you in there?"

"You're causing a scene. I'd like it if you left," Wendy tried to say over my shouting.

"It's not your house. You have no right to tell me to go." I tried to catch a look in the front window. "Sally, it's me, Kath!"

"Look, she's really not here." Wendy stepped down onto the path, and I actually thought I saw sadness in her eyes. "The doctor said no one can visit, not for a few more days. If you like I will notify you when you can go to see her."

"What about the kids? Are they okay?"

Wendy drew in a deep breath. Was she trying to stifle tears? She looked at me, her eyes shiny. "I'm staying here with them. They don't need to be any more unsettled than they already are."

I took a step back, unaccustomed to a Wendy who showed emotions. "You promise me you'll let me know when I can visit?" I found an old receipt in the bottom of my bag and jotted my number on the back. "Please keep me informed. I love her too, you know."

Wendy nodded and took the scrap of paper from me.

"Will you give the kiddies a hug from their Auntie Kathy?"

Wendy nodded again, and this time she couldn't disguise the tears in her eyes.

I turned and left, the guilt at not being there for Sally eating up my insides. She must have gone down again after I'd seen her last week. How stupid of me for thinking she'd got it beat. I slammed my hand against the steering wheel. Hurry up, Bob. Work out those little nanoparticles you seem to love so much and help Jimmy fix the damn machine.

TWENTY-TWO

Results Day

I'd gone to sleep with a headache. Sleep was the wrong term to use. I tossed and turned and wished for sleep and a head that didn't feel like it was about to burst. Thursday morning arrived and I woke up seriously thinking one of my eyes was going to pop out. I held a hand over that eye and rustled around in the medicines' drawer in my bedside cabinet, grabbing both the Paracetamol and ibuprofen. The pain had manifested as a balloon-like pressure that lived just behind my forehead. I took the medicines, swallowing the handful of pills with a swig of the still too-hot tea Jimmy had brought me, but they didn't seem to ease the pain in the slightest.

What would I do if my eye did pop out? Call 999? Run screaming to Jimmy? I pictured myself tearing around the house cupping an escaped eyeball in one hand, and Jimmy running after me with his trusty toolbox. The pills must have been taking effect. The pressure eased up just a shade and my eye stopped feeling like it was about to burst free. I glanced at the clock. Less than an hour to go before the appointment. I didn't really see the point in making sure we were on time, the doc was always at least an hour behind, even if we were the first people on the list. I knew why and didn't feel resentment towards Mr. Noble. He invariably got caught up on the wards with patients who were arguably in a far worse state than me.

I climbed out of bed as Jimmy exited the bathroom, clutching my stomach as it did a roll. It wasn't the cancer that was going to kill me, it was the stress before these result appointments that would get me. Friends of mine on a bowel cancer forum had even coined a word for it: scanxiety.

We got to the outpatients' department in Clatterbridge right on time. Jimmy and I weren't really talking much. We'd gone through the possible results we might get as we always did as we drove to the hospital. The way we saw it, these were the outcomes; firstly, the tumors would be unchanged. Secondly, there'd be some reduction. Lastly, the tumors would be bigger and in more places. We didn't dare entertain the chance the pod had done some good to me.

We sat down in the waiting area. Three roof lights created an atrium-like feel, with three groupings of chairs under each light. Consulting rooms ringed the chairs. I grabbed a magazine and opened it, not reading the pages, just staring at Mr. Noble's door, willing it to open and for his nurse, Jill to appear and call us in. Jimmy sat next to me, not even taking his phone out. The two of us sat like that, fixated on the door as other patients trickled in and the waiting room slowly filled.

"Kathy?" The voice came from behind.

I turned and found Jill looking out from a room I'd not been in before.

"Do you want to come through?"

I tossed the magazine back on the table and Jimmy and I followed her, taking a seat in the chairs beside the examination bed.

Jill sat in a chair opposite. "Mr. Noble is really sorry, he's been called away on an emergency. But he felt it was really important for you to get your results today, so we've kept your appointment and you'll be seeing Dr. Saechao instead. Is this okay or would you rather reschedule?"

Jimmy and I exchanged a look. I read the same feelings in him as I had in myself. "I'll see this other doctor. Not sure I can survive waiting any longer." I tried to laugh, but my nerves were shot and I was sure I sounded like a mad scientist.

We were used to Mr. Noble and his balmy way of handling appointments. After more than two years I knew what my results would be just by the way he walked into the room.

Dr. I'd-forgotten-his-name-already walked into the room. Instead of our tall, Swedish-looking doc with a ready smile and happy nature, we had a petite Asian doctor with a blank face. He shook our hands and didn't even bother to sit. He laid a folder with my notes on the bed and glanced at them.

How bad would it be? Was my time of thinking me cured or nearly-cured up? I'd end up with Sally this time. Last time the darkness descended was after my cancelled surgery. I should have been admitted. Even

Jimmy said so after weeks passed and the dark veil began to lift, and we realized just how bad I'd been.

The doctor didn't mince his words and told us straight. "I've got the results of your latest scan here." He flicked through several images. He settled on one of my lungs. "This latest combination of drugs has been very effective. You no longer seem to have any tumors in your lungs."

I felt Jimmy's hand on my leg. He squeezed hard. Tears sprang, and I blinked and tried to stop them with some controlled breaths.

"In your previous scan we found eighteen tumors in your liver. We can only find two now, and the two remaining are down from 36mm and 32mm to 18mm and 10mm." He shuffled through the scan pictures. "You have had an amazing response to the latest course of chemotherapy, and Mr. Noble has suggested that surgery might be an option again."

Tears really fell now. I wiped at my cheeks, and nodded, unable to speak. Jill passed over a box of tissues and I grabbed a couple. Surgery, a magical word that I'd been told would never again be open to me. I held onto Jimmy's hand, not daring to look his way.

"We're sending your file to Mr. Wright, over at Aintree."

That was our liver specialist. The one who had cancelled my surgery at the last minute a year earlier. I'd been deemed too unstable and no longer operable. That was the day I went from having hope to being classed as incurable.

"Your case will be discussed at the next MDT meeting."

Doctor whoever-he-was looked to me to try and judge my reaction to the news. I give him a thumbs up and tried to stifle my sobs. I'd be discussed at the MDT, that meeting where all the docs got together and decided the best course of action for patients.

More things were said, but I'd stopped listening. All I could hear was the word *surgery*. Jimmy and I kind of floated out of the room after the meeting ended. The carrot of living was being dangled in front of me and the tears just wouldn't stop falling. We went for a cup of tea in the Clatterbridge café. I needed to gather myself.

Of course this meant far more than the doctors here realized. This wasn't about a course of chemo that miraculously worked. This was the proof I needed, *the pod worked*. It was a lifesaver. Somehow, between Jimmy and Bob they had to work out the secrets and fix the machine.

A friend had told me a quote by Dennis Potter after his terminal cancer diagnosis. He'd said the blossom that spring was the blossomest blossom he'd ever seen. Since I heard this, I'd been searching for the same beauty, and had come to the conclusion that this was a lie. Everything turned to shades of grey for me. Maybe this man did see the blossomest blossom. But for me, with the possibility of life being given back to me suddenly, through the tears that still wouldn't stop, it was like a light turned on. *Now* I saw the blossomest blossom. And the leafiest leaves and the bluest of skies and the puffiest clouds and everything around me was extra bright and extra colorful, everything, everywhere and all at once.

And the thought that came to mind was, *thank you, Janie.*

Jimmy and I took our time going home, making a detour to Ness Botanical Gardens and walking around in silence. My tears didn't stop for a long time, and I earned looks of sympathy from some of the elderly ladies we passed. Jimmy held my hand, his grip tight as he stared into the distance, off in his own world. Maybe he was daring to plan our future again. Maybe he was thinking about Bob and how far he'd got in figuring out the nanoparticles. Maybe he was doing the same as me – adjusting his mind to the realization that not only did the pod actually, positively, and categorically work, but that it had *almost* fixed me. Even if the machine never worked again, I got to have another bite at the apple. I had a chance to have new treatments that might finish the job the machine started. Oh, to dare to hope.

We arrived home late in the afternoon. Jimmy went straight back to work, not bothering to use his headphones and filling the house with Rush played at high volume. The phone rang, and in a daze, I picked up.

"Hello?"

"Kathy, it's your dad. Your mother told me about this machine. I have to say I did think she was having a turn. Is it true?"

I nodded, tears threatening again. God how I hated to cry, I hated the way it made me feel weak and out of control. I drew in a ragged breath and managed to say, "Yup."

"A machine from the future is real?"

"Yes Dad." I stretched the phone cord to the downstairs loo and splashed a little water on my face. "It's all true, Dad. Jimmy *had* to have a look inside the works and managed to break a part. We've got someone looking into it."

"Well, I'll be honest with you, that's why I phoned. You see, one of my mates down the boatyard works in the aerospace industry. He's a precision machinist. I reckon if anyone can fix your machine he can." Dad paused. "Kathy, are you okay?"

I sniffed, and said, "Uh-huh."

"Did something happen?"

"I got my scan results today." Breathe in, breathe out, I forced slow deep breaths, trying desperately to keep my emotions in check. Stop falling apart, I told myself.

"Oh no…"

"No, it's not like that, Dad. They were good, really good. My lungs are clear and I'm down to two tumors in my liver."

My words were met with what I could only describe as stunned silence. Dad always had something to say. Him being silent said more than words. Then he was speaking again, "That's wonderful! Mary, Mary, come to the phone!" Dad shouted. I held the handset away from my ear as he yelled a second time. "Come hear Kath's news!"

Finally my tears cleared. This was the beginning, a bright new start. I spoke with Mum and at Dad's insistence arranged to meet him at the church in an hour. He wanted to assess the damage. I decided not to tell Jimmy, he'd only feel hurt that I was recruiting Dad to clean up his mess.

I had told Dad to park in the council car park. The lot was mostly empty when I arrived. The shops had closed now, only a few restaurants were open at this time of the evening. Dad drove up and saw me waving. He pulled into the space next to my car.

"Bit cloak and dagger this," he said as he joined me.

"I'm supposed to be fixed by now, and should probably have passed the key onto the next person."

Dad frowned. "So does it only fix one person at a time?"

"I don't think so. The machine seems so advanced, I imagine it can fix queues of people."

"So why limit it like this, having only one person at a time getting the benefit?"

I linked arms with my dad and we started walking around the shops to get to the church.

"I don't know. I didn't make the rules." The church came into view, looking as grimy and neglected as always. "You see what you make of it, Dad."

I wrangled with the lock and opened the door wide. Dad stood still for a minute, staring first at the cross, then at the shiny pod in the middle of the floor. He didn't say a word, and moved slowly into the church, glancing at the piles of pews on either side of the space. Then as he came up to the pod, he reached out and ran his fingertips over the hull as he circled it.

"So smooth," he muttered. He'd got round to the back where the panel remained open from Jimmy's last visit. "I see, I see." Dad mumbled to himself.

I sat on a pew behind him and watched as he examined the mechanics. He put his hand up to the broken pipe, running his fingers over the places Jimmy had used solder to seal the breaks.

"Hmm, cold." He leaned closer and sniffed. "Yes, I know what that is." He backed off and lay down, looking into the machinery from another angle. "That's why the seal's not working." Dad sat back up. "Lend me the key. I can have the break fixed by the end of the weekend."

"Seriously, fixed that soon?"

"Oh yes, it's a simple fix. Jimmy was part of the way there, but he's used the wrong material for the solder." He scratched at his beard. "It won't be working, but it will be mended. You say you've got a man working on the gas that escaped?"

"Yes…"

"Tell him that the pressure is probably maintained by nitrogen vapor."

I blinked slowly. I knew Dad was intelligent, but he'd worked in engineering. How did he know this stuff? "What about your friend?"

Dad didn't reply at first, he was staring deep inside the machine. Everything was shiny and smooth, no greasy or oily parts that I could see. Without looking back at me he made a 'don't worry' gesture with his hand. "No need to involve him. I have a question about a valve, but I don't need Tim here to get the answer." He nodded, still concentrating on the mechanics. "The fewer people that know about this beauty the better."

"Yes, of course. That's why Jimmy and I have been trying to keep things quiet."

That Elusive Cure

"That's my girl," Dad said and got up off the floor. He brushed the dust off his trousers. "Can I hold onto the key? I'll give it back as soon as I've done my bit."

I hesitated. Last time someone got a hold of the key bad things happened. But this was my dad, the man that could fix anything. I handed it over. The machine was already broken. What more could go wrong?

Before we left, I went to the front of the pod and touched the side to open the lid. Dad stood back, watching as it silently pivoted up. Once it stopped moving, I reached up into the lid and placed my hand on the panel. Maybe it had a way of recharging itself. I held my breath and waited for the soft voice of the machine.

"Come on, Kath, your mother will be wondering where I am."

The lid automatically began to lower again.

"Coming," I said and followed him out of the church, looking one last time at the machine before locking the door.

TWENTY-THREE

Bob Gives an Update

We woke to the sound of the phone ringing. Squinting at the clock, I realized it was only four in the morning. I threw the covers off and ran for the phone. I could only think of one reason why the phone would ring at such an early hour: bad news.

"Yes?" I stood on the landing, out of breath. Through the open door I could see Jimmy sitting up in bed looking worried.

"I've got news!"

A second passed before I could figure out who was on the line, and why I'd want news in the middle of the night.

"I think I might be able to produce more. At first I thought I'd be able to using radiation chemistry. Oh, and it has a polymeric coating. This is good, it's highly stable."

It was Bob, tripping over his words in effort to get them out as fast as possible. I let out a sigh of relief. No one was injured or dying. I waved Jimmy over. "Hold on, Bob, I'm putting you on speaker phone."

He didn't pause to even acknowledge me. "More rudimentary coatings have been developed already, but nothing as advanced as this." Bob sounded very excited. "The coating suggests this nanoparticle is being used for an organic reaction. I was right, this is for a medicinal application."

"We did tell you that when you were here," I said.

"Yes, yes you did. But the first rule of unknown substances is not to give credence to any information given." He barely paused for breath. "But that's not the exciting part. I'll give you a little background. Common address tags are monoclonal antibodies, aptamers, streptavidin or peptides. What we normally like to see is these targeting agents covalently linked to the nanoparticle."

"Hang on, I don't understand what you're saying."

Bob sighed, "Which bit?"

I didn't like to say all of it, so I picked the last part. "Look, you woke us up and my brain is only partially functioning, you have to give us a little leeway here, okay? That part about the links, what does that mean?"

"A covalent link is when there is a chemical bond shared between the particles…"

"Okay, that's enough for me. You'll just confuse me if you say more. Continue." I ignored Jimmy as he suppressed a laugh.

Bob started speaking again, a slight hurt tone to his voice. "Where was I… right, the targeting agents should be present in a controlled number per nanoparticle. The particles you sent me are multivalent nanoparticles. That means they have multiple targeting groups. This is important as they can cluster receptors and activate cellular signaling pathways."

Christ, I didn't understand a word he was saying. Jimmy shrugged and gave me an equally confused look.

Bob forged on. "This gives them stronger anchoring. The particles also have a red blood cell coating. This helps the nanoparticles evade the immune system."

Jimmy cleared his throat and said, "So you're getting closer to figuring our little baby out?"

"Oh, definitely. But that's not the reason I phoned. Do you have any idea how much research is going on in this field right now? It's where all the big money is being spent. But the results haven't been terrific and the particles tend to be cytotoxic."

"What's that?" I asked.

"Like chemotherapy, it poisons the patient while making them better."

"Oh…"

"But I don't think that's the case with my beautiful little particle."

Jimmy and I exchanged a look, both of us picking up on his sudden ownership of our nanoparticle.

"Then I discovered it is a grey goo replicator."

"Grey goo…?" Jimmy echoed.

"Yes, this is so exciting. Grey goo is like the bogeyman to scientists. It's long been feared by us. Think of that old movie The Blob. A carbon-eating nanoparticle escapes and slowly eats up all the carbon in the world as it replicates."

"And that's what grey goo is?" I asked.

That Elusive Cure

"It's when a particle uses carbon as a food source to replicate. The resulting mass, if you like, is called grey goo."

"Aren't we made of carbon?" Jimmy said.

I glanced at him, thinking excellent point. A thought came to me; this particle was presumably made in the future. Maybe they had ways of controlling it that Bob didn't know about or simply hadn't been invented yet. Visions of healthy people being eaten up by blob-like infestations flashed through my mind.

"Oh yes, but that's the beauty of this particle." He paused as if for effect. "And this is the reason I'm calling now. My discovery just couldn't wait. It took me all night, but I found the only way it will replicate is with a very specific electrical charge being applied, and only for a very specific amount of time. If it could replicate freely what you'd end up with is the nightmare scenario of grey goo growing freely as the nanoparticles consumed the world."

For a moment no one said anything.

Then Jimmy said, "Does that mean you can make more?"

"Don't get ahead of yourself, I'm not there yet, but my initial estimate of two years is way off. Give me maybe nine months and I think I'll be making endless supplies of this stuff. At the moment I can only make it reproduce in a very limited fashion."

"This is wonderful," I said quietly.

"Fantastic work, Bob. Let us know if you make any more discoveries," Jimmy added.

I put the phone down, feeling numb. Maybe this would all work out. I crossed my fingers and toes and looked up to see Jimmy beaming widely.

"This is amazing," he said. "He's actually figuring it out."

I nodded, tears in my eyes. Words wouldn't come, just a sob that came from deep inside of me. Jimmy wrapped me up in his arms.

"Shush, shush. See, I told you it would all be okay." He rubbed my back, rocking me as the tears fell.

I pulled back, and still unable to speak I gave him a thumbs up and a weak smile.

"The machine *will* work again. I promise you," Jimmy said and pulled me tighter.

I pictured the last tumors left inside me. Was their time up? Yes, I decided. The countdown had begun.

TWENTY-FOUR

Dad and the Machine

Dad had left a message on the phone saying he'd be heading over to the church Saturday afternoon. I wanted to be there. I trusted Dad, but I'd trusted Jimmy as well, and that hadn't ended well.

I set off, the summer had taken a turn and it almost felt autumnal. Dad's car was in the council lot again, and I found a spot near to him and got out, the wind bashing me as I walked to the church. Litter raced past me and I struggled to keep my hair out of my face. Bob's call the morning before had left me emotional again. My hatred of being out of control colored my day dull. The clouds raced past, barely giving the sun more than the odd moment to shine through. The expanse of grey above me didn't help my mood.

The door to the church was locked. I banged on the door and thought I heard a "hello?" through the wood.

"It's me, Kath," I called out.

I waited, watching the traffic driving past and feeling exposed. My treatment should be finished.

What if this Richard Newland kept tabs on his church? What if he drove by regularly noting the users? My guess would be he had the master key and the one I currently had in my possession was a duplicate. Maybe he'd been in the church when we weren't here and already knew of the mess we'd made of his miraculous pod.

The door swung open and Dad greeted me with a grin. "You'll never guess what I figured out."

Well, if this wasn't going to be another day for discoveries. I stood next to him as he locked the door again, staring not at the pod but the cross above. Jesus hung off the wood, eyes closed and an expression of suffering on his face. His arms stretched out, the pressure of his body pulling forward bringing the sinews out. Did he have a pod hidden away in that cave? I made a quick sign of the cross, thinking that was sacrilege of the highest order, and I needed everything in my favor, even the opinion of a god far above me.

Dad gave me a brief shoulder squashing hug and pulled me towards the machine. "Ready to guess what I found out today?"

I shrugged and gave him my best sarcastic look. "That the machine works with pixie dust?"

"Better." His grin widened. "Check this out." He went behind the machine and closed the panel.

"Power restarting. Diagnostics initiating." The machine spoke!

I ran around to the other side of the pod and triggered the lid to open. As it opened I knelt down, resting my hands on the mattress. The foam grabbed onto me as I listened for more.

"Pressure in the nanoparticle chamber is 60% and not high enough for functionality. Recommend recharging the system with nitrogen vapor. Nanoparticle density is 45% and not high enough for functionality. Recommend recharging with MicroHealth nanoparticles. Please contact MicroHealth representative for necessary repairs."

"See, I was right." Dad had come around behind me. I glanced up at him. He looked proud. "I fixed the leak properly and installed a new valve. I'm not going to risk ferreting around inside searching for the proper one."

"But she spoke!"

"Yes, well," he came over a little sheepish, "that I discovered by accident. My valve fix was a little cumbersome, so I had to make sure the panel would close. When I did, the lady started up."

I let out a small laugh.

"Scared the life out of me when she spoke. You could have warned me."

"This is amazing." I slipped off my shoes and climbed into the pod. "Do you suppose the scanner still works?"

"Since you've not told me anything, and the info I do have is second-hand off your mother, I wouldn't have the first clue what the machine does or doesn't do even when it is working."

I rolled my eyes at Dad, making sure he noticed. "The machine scans you and then fixes you using those little nanoparticles. If there's power I don't see why it can't scan people still. I wanted to know if the MRI and this thing matched up. Having the same results would be the final acknowledgment that the machine really worked.

Dad poked the mattress. "Fascinating," he said as it swelled around his finger.

"You think that's fascinating, watch this." I reached up and put my hand on the panel.

The lid began slowly closing. I grinned at Dad until the lid clicked closed.

The machine started speaking, "Patient recognized. Scan initiating."

Thank God. I snuggled into the mattress. The machine still worked, I couldn't believe it. Should have got my father in on the fix days ago.

"Diagnosing."

Would the pod match up with what the MRI saw?

"Two tumors found in the liver of 19mm and 10mm. Left and right lung now clear."

One millimeter difference in the measurements, but otherwise identical to what that doctor told us at Clatterbridge. I felt the excitement building in me. If we could get some of that gas and refill the system the machine could finish the job it started. My thoughts were interrupted by the pod-voice.

"Three sessions of the four recommended have been completed. Sessions can be resumed after required maintenance."

"End session?" the machine asked.

"Yes," I said and the lid began opening.

I smiled as Dad's face came into view.

"Speechless, Dad? Astounded? It's pretty amazing, isn't it?"

Dad's mouth worked, but no words came out. "We need to fix this miracle," he finally said.

That Elusive Cure

He took my hands and helped me out of the pod.

"Do you think I could have a go? I mean, I feel fine, but it would be good to have a body scan. At my age you can never be certain of anything." A rose tint grew on his cheeks.

I glanced back at the pod. "Don't see why not…"

"You don't think it'll mess up your sessions?" He placed his hand on the mattress, pulling away as it tried to grab on.

"Things are already messed up, Dad. Go for it."

I sat on a pew as Dad took off his shoes and climbed carefully in.

"Don't worry about the mattress. It's like memory foam, kind of. It won't swallow you or anything like that."

Dad lay down. "You sure about that, I swear it's trying to eat me."

I laughed. "Stop being a baby and lie down."

He settled down and stared at the lid. "What do I do, say *close sesame* or something?"

Shaking my head and trying not to laugh more, I pointed to the panel above him. "Put your hand on that. It'll close then."

"Okay…" He reached up tentatively and spread his left hand on the smooth metal. The lid immediately began to close. Dad lay there, arms stiff at his sides, not far off a state of terror and I remembered all that medicine it pumped into me to calm me down. Would that still be working?

The lid clicked closed and as clearly as if I'd heard it inside the pod, the voice said, "Heartbeat and blood pressure raised. Antihypertensive being administered."

That must have come from a different system to the nanoparticles. How many kinds of medicines did this thing have stored in it?

"Patient registered via DNA. Scan initiating." *

Even out here, sat on a dusty pew the soft words of the woman relaxed me.

"Diagnosing."

I suppose she'd find some arthritis. Dad was seventy-nine years old. Surely he'd have a couple of age-related issues to fix. The machine seemed to be taking ages. I sat waiting, picking my nails and tapping my foot.

Finally, the voice stated up again. "Tumor found in the prostate measuring 4mm."

Oh my god. No, not my dad. I sat stiffly on the pew.

"Two sessions recommended. Sessions can begin after required maintenance. End session?"

Dad mustn't have realized he needed to respond, and the voice spoke again.

"End session?"

This time I heard Dad say, "Yes."

The lid popped open and slowly rose. Dad didn't move, his face pale and slack. I guessed I probably looked similar.

"Oh, Dad. I'm so sorry."

He sat up, the color already returning to his face. "It's not that much of a surprise. I'm sure I read that any man who lives to one-hundred will have developed prostate cancer."

"Don't be so flip, Dad. This is too serious for jokes."

"No it isn't," he said, his tone sharp. "It's my body, I can joke about any problems I have if I choose to."

"Okay, fine."

"And 4mm is tiny. Even if this magic machine of yours never works again, I can get the doc to lop the thing out of me." He held one of his hands up and held his thumb and finger slightly apart. "That's all it is. Like one of those a petit pois peas your mother likes."

The air in the church suddenly felt cloying, I had to get out. I thought for a second, I didn't need to just get out. I needed ice cream. And not just ice cream, I needed a great big sundae with a mountain of whipped cream and hot fudge and caramel sauce.

"Come on, Dad. Want to drown your sorrows with me? We can be depressed cancer buddies."

He looked sideways at me. "The pub?"

"No, silly. Much better than the pub. Ice cream."

TWENTY-FIVE

Visiting Wendy

As I walked up to Sally's house and heard shrieks of laughter, I couldn't help but think, just for one moment, that maybe Wendy had done the right thing putting Sally away. Then the betrayal of my thoughts took over. Sally was locked away, and it was all her sister's fault.

The doorbell echoed through the house, and I stood back, enjoying the early morning sunshine on my face. The door opened and Peter and Lucy barreled out at me.

"Auntie Kathy!" Peter shrieked. Even Lucy let out a giggle. The pair of them clung to me like limpets. Behind them, Wendy waited just inside the house.

"Do you want to come in?" she asked.

I nodded. "Just need to manhandle these two in." The three of us waddled inside the house. I shook them off onto the floor where they lay in a giggling heap for a second before jumping up and bolting out the backdoor and into the garden.

"Such a difference in them." I had to say it. It was as if entirely different kids were in the house.

That Elusive Cure

Wendy acknowledged my words with a slight smile. What if I'd given her ammunition against her sister: *Even your best friend thinks you do a rubbish job raising your kids.* Is that what she'd say to Sal?

"Would you like a drink? The kettle just boiled."

I glanced at the door, before turning back to Wendy. "That would be lovely. Any news?"

"Nothing to get your hopes up yet."

I followed Wendy to the kitchen and leaned against a countertop while she busied herself making tea.

"She's still not allowed phone calls, but you can send a letter. I had the kids send in drawings."

I was supposed to hate Wendy, like a mutual hate pact or something. Sally hated her, so I should hate her. But somehow I couldn't help but warm to this silver-haired version of my best friend.

"Do you reckon they check the letters? You know, before they hand them over."

Wendy shrugged. "Would make sense, I guess." She gave the teapot a stir before deciding it ready. "Why, are you planning on writing something that might upset her?"

"No…" I thought of how insane the pod would sound on paper. "Just need to word things in a way that they let it through, that's all."

Wendy loaded up a tray and went through to the living room. She poured my tea and topped up the cup with a drop of milk. I didn't even know Sally had china like this. Maybe Wendy brought her own from home? There was a couple who came to the husband's chemo sessions at Clatterbridge with a thermos of tea, which wasn't so unusual, but also their own china cups. Made me smile every time I saw them. It was a comfort thing, and maybe this was Wendy's way of easing a difficult situation.

"I've been keeping Sally updated on the situation with the children. I go and drop the letters off by hand and according to the nurse they've been getting through."

The hospital was nearly an hour's drive away. That was some commitment, taking them by hand.

Wendy sipped at her tea and I realized just how polar this was to my typical visits to this house. Normally Sal and I used giant mugs, and ate sticky cakes and laughed constantly at each other's silliness. It was all too serious for me. I finished my tea, said my thanks and went out to the garden to see the kids.

Peter and Lucy were playing on a trampoline I'd never seen before, the breathy squeaks of the springs in perfect sync with the kids' shrieks and screams of laughter.

"See you guys later," I called out and was rewarded with the pair of them shouting out goodbyes. Even Lucy was talking. Damn, this was going to be hard on them when Sally came back. I was sure they missed their mother, and I almost hated seeing them this happy. It kind of reinforced how bad a job of motherhood Sal was doing.

I got home and took a pad of paper from a cupboard. Staring at the blank page wasn't making my thoughts any less confused. I got up and made a cup of tea – a proper cup of tea using the biggest mug in the cabinet. I raised the cup to Sal before taking the first sip. Where was she now? Locked up in her room? Wandering around a common area? I'd never been to a psych ward. Sal had never wanted to talk about her visits once she was home, so I only had movies and TV programs to base my ideas on. Were there metal grates separating the staff from the patients? Lots of locked doors and screwed-down chairs and tables?

Getting my thoughts in order finally, I started my letter.

Hey Sally,

It's all gone to shit. Found out my dad's got prostate cancer. It's this tiny little tumor, really early stages. The docs should cut it out and hopefully that'll be the end of it. The shittiest part is I can't explain to you why this is so bad and why I'm not entirely happy that my lungs came up clear in the last scan. Yes, you read right. Plus, I've only got two tumors in my liver, and yet I'm not jumping for joy. There's big things going on in my life and if I told anyone I'd end up in there with you in the next bed. Jesus. It's all messed up.

I'll tell you this. Got this new scanner. It's so accurate that I'm afraid to let my mum go in it because I'm terrified of what they'll find. Me, I'm a walking poster child for ignoring symptoms. I should be shouting at people to get the scan. The sooner you know, the better the chances, and yet it's all bullshit.

Saw your kids today. Wendy's doing a good job with them. They miss you so much, though. Get better for them and come home soon. Hell, I need you. You and me have some serious catching up to do and I need you here.

I'm not making any sense, so I'm going to stop while I'm way behind. Get better. I need you.

Kath xxx

That would have to do. I sealed it in an envelope, and decided I needed some time to clear my head. I'd hand deliver the letter like Wendy did. Maybe I could find out some information about Sal while I was there. Hell, I was practically family; I deserved to know how she was.

I dipped into the garage where Jimmy was working on a shelving project. "I'm going to drop this off for Sally." I waved the letter in the air.

Jimmy grunted at me. He was obviously still miffed at me for letting my dad do the fix on the machine. Grow up, I thought, it's not all about you.

"See you later," I said when it was obvious he wasn't going to talk to me.

I walked down the driveway and got in the car, hoping I'd find Jimmy at the window, knocking on the glass for me to open up and give him a kiss, but he stayed hidden in the garage. Jesus, life's too short for this. But that didn't stop me putting the car in gear and driving off.

TWENTY-SIX

Nanoparticle Miracles

I didn't get to see Sally. No visits allowed, I was told. Can't disclose information to a non-relative. We'll see she gets the letter. I heard the nurse rip into the envelope as I left the reception area. Would my words pass and be handed on? I'd find out eventually, I hoped.

Jimmy called Bob on Sunday, told him we needed nitrogen vapor, and could he get some for us. Of course this started a big debate. Bob wouldn't just supply it, he had to bring it and only *he* could handle the canister. Bob didn't get an immediate answer. I made Jimmy hang up and convince me this wasn't a stupid thing to do. Jimmy and I discussed the issue of Bob seeing the machine for near on an hour. We decided to allow him into the church, but it was going to be a cloak and dagger affair. We'd blindfold him and take him there.

I heard Bob before I saw him. His old red Fiesta came grumbling up the street. Nerves were getting to me, and I sat by the window, watching as Bob eased his car up onto the pavement in front of my house.

The Fiesta belched blue smoke out the exhaust as he turned her off.

Bob got out, lanky and disheveled in an ancient once-white t-shirt and possibly the same pair of jeans as last time. He opened the boot, put on a pair of thick gloves and lifted out a reasonably-sized grey metal canister. It must have been heavy, as he turned my way I watched his face scrunch up from the effort. The canister clanked as he placed it on the pavement.

Jimmy walked down the driveway to meet Bob. The two of them moved the canister into the boot of Jimmy's car and then came inside.

"Hi, how are you?" Bob's face was flushed from the exertion. "So, exactly what is the nitrogen vapor needed for?"

Jimmy glanced at me and indicated I should do the talking. Bob would see the machine soon enough, but it was still hard to give up its secrets to this relative stranger.

"We've got a machine, it has those nanoparticles inside it." I checked with Jimmy, he gave me an encouraging look. "We'll take you to it, but it's all top secret. So you'll have to be blindfolded."

"Who invented the machine? Can't be either of you or you wouldn't have needed to come to me."

"How very astute."

"You said I had to go blindfolded? Real spy stuff going on. What are you afraid of?"

Did that really need to be said out loud? Did he really need me to explain my fears? Sometimes I wondered how smart people could be so stupid. I picked up a scarf from the sofa beside me. "Can you sit?"

Bob shifted from one foot to the other. "Seriously, blindfolded? I won't look. I'll keep my eyes closed. There's no need for that."

Jimmy stepped closer. "Look, without the blindfold you don't get to see the machine. And believe me, this thing is like nothing you've ever seen before. You want to see it. Trust me."

Bob hesitated then perched on the arm of the sofa. "Okay, I guess…"

"You're making the right choice," I said and wrapped the scarf around his head.

Hoping none of the neighbors happened to be out on the street Jimmy and I led Bob to the car and got him safely onto the back seat. The last part of our security plan was to make him lie down. Hopefully this would be enough to keep the location of the church a secret.

Jimmy drove and the three of us remained silent for the journey. To be honest the whole situation was surreal. I felt like I was taking part in a movie and didn't know it. For goodness sake, we had a genius scientist blindfolded and lying down on the back seat! How very strange my life had become.

The church seemed to loom at us as Jimmy pulled into the tiny car park.

"Stay there a minute. I'm going to unlock the door," I told Bob. "Jimmy will stay with you."

"Not planning on murdering me are you?" Bob said and laughed nervously.

"Not today, anyway," I replied, probably not helping his nerves, but I couldn't help myself.

Jimmy laughed as I got out. Before going to the church, I checked the street briefly. Who or what was

I looking for? Not entirely sure I crossed the small car park to the entrance and wrestled with the lock once more, opening the door wide. My eyes rested on the pod for a moment before indicating at Jimmy to come.

We led Bob into the church and sat him on a pew while Jimmy donned the thick gloves and retrieved the canister from the boot of the car. He staggered inside with it as I locked up.

"You can take the scarf off now," I told Bob.

He couldn't get it off fast enough. Bob blinked in the light, squinting and frowning as he tried to understand where he was and what he was looking at. I watched amazement dawn on him. Bob looked from the pod to the cross to the piles of pews to the pod to Jimmy and then me and back to the pod where they stayed.

"What on earth…" He got up and approached slowly.

I beamed, feeling stupidly like a proud mother. This wasn't *my* machine, I needed to remember that. This was a machine I was invited to use and then pass on to another needy person. My smile grew wider as the scientist circled the room, his eyes not leaving the pod.

"Amazing, isn't it?" Jimmy asked before crouching down at the back.

Bob nodded, words evading him as he reached out and touched the smooth metal.

"Come have a look at this."

Bob went around to where Jimmy was and I watched his eyes widen. "Wow," he said finally. "Just wow."

He sat on the floor next to Jimmy, hardly even blinking. His eyes darted around, making me think he was soaking up all the details he could. Maybe Bob had a photographic memory. If he remembered the way the innards of the machine were, what harm could it cause us and this machine? Feeling a little uneasy I got up and stood behind him. "Shouldn't we be topping up the gas?"

"It's a vapor," Bob told me with a wave of his hand.

"Same bloody difference," I said, but neither of them was listening. "Just top up the *vapor* and let's get out of here. I don't want to be in here any longer than we need to."

"Can you bring the canister; I want to study this a little longer."

Jimmy got up and hefted the container over. Bob seemed done with his mind snapshots or whatever he was up to and the two of them hooked up the pipe to the valve my father had installed.

"You two might want to step back in case there's a leak or something."

"Not going to blow it up, are you." Jimmy laughed, but stepped back nonetheless.

"No chance. But the cold burns. You wouldn't want that."

I sat on a pew, curling my legs up under me and waiting for Bob to do his bit. How would he know when it was full? What if he overfilled the system and damaged it even more? Feeling a distinct lack of control over the pod and the journey I had unwittingly caused it, I hugged my arms around me and did the only thing I could. I hoped for the best.

Bob attached the tube from the canister to the pipe on the pod. With his thick gloves back on, he slowly turned the release valve. I'd done a little research and now knew that this was the stuff they put in those fancy cocktails in some of the bars in Liverpool. Some people had been hurt by it. The stuff was cold, so cold it froze anything.

Jimmy stood to the side of me, watching intently as Bob turned the valve another notch. "How will you know when it's full?"

"I'm not sure. The tubing might pop off. That's why I asked you to stand away."

A vision of the church with a layer of freezing fog hiding the floor made me think of music videos from the 80s. Just needed Duran Duran to come in and blast out one of the early techno songs.

"I know how to test it." Of course, I had the answer all along. "Turn off the nitrogen stuff and take off the tubing."

"And why would I do that?" Bob seemed irritated. I wondered if I'd interrupted further mental mapping of the insides of the pod. To be honest, I was surprised he'd not taken out his phone and snapped a few shots on the camera.

"Because if you close the hatch at the back the machine will talk and tell you how much it needs."

Bob frowned. "Exactly where did this machine come from?"

"Look, just do as I say."

Bob turned the valve to stop the vapor and removed the tube. Jimmy came up behind him and showed the scientist how to close the panel and reseal the machine.

"Power restarting. Diagnostics initiating." My lovely machine started up.

Unsure of where to put himself, Bob backed up, listening for more.

"Pressure in the nanoparticle chamber is 60% and not high enough for functionality. Recommend recharging the system with nitrogen vapor. Nanoparticle density is 50% and not high enough for functionality. Recommend recharging with MicroHealth nanoparticles. Please contact MicroHealth representative for necessary repairs."

"Wow," Bob said. "This has to be from the future. You know what this means? A discovery like this? It'll change the views of the world. It'll *heal* the world." He brushed his hand along the smooth hull. "If this confirms actual time travel…" His voice petered off as he circled around to the back. "You two at a safe distance?"

"Yup," I said and watched from the pew as Bob set up the vapor for a second time. He filled for a timed minute then closed it down again, shut the panel and listened for the machine's voice.

"Power restarting. Diagnostics initiating."

Bob stayed where he was this time and listened.

"Pressure in the nanoparticle chamber is 65% and not high enough for functionality. Recommend recharging the system with nitrogen vapor. Nanoparticle density is 50% and not high enough for functionality. Recommend recharging with MicroHealth nanoparticles. Please contact MicroHealth representative for necessary repairs."

The scientist muttered to himself for a second, then reattached the canister and set the timer on his watch going as he turned the release valve. We sat in silence as Bob pumped in the gas. It didn't take long for me to get bored of watching him, and my attention turned to the cross. The sun was skimming the top of the building across the road and coming through the top of the stained glass windows. Despite the layers of dirt I could still pick out colors as they covered Christ in a rainbow. Made me want to pay a window cleaner, I wanted to see the church bathed in color.

I was about to say as much to Jimmy when Bob's watch beeped. For a third time he shut down the process and closed the hatch.

"Power restarting. Diagnostics initiating."

Would it be enough? I tapped my fingers on the wood, waiting for the answer.

"Pressure in the nanoparticle chamber is 92% and not high enough for functionality. Recommend recharging the system with nitrogen vapor. Nanoparticle density is 50% and not high enough for functionality. Recommend recharging with MicroHealth nanoparticles. Please contact MicroHealth representative for necessary repairs."

"I'm playing it safe," Bob said. "I'll go slow from here. My guess is the machine has a tolerance. If I can charge the system to the point where that tolerance is reached then that part of the machine will be operable again. Then it's up to me to produce more of the nanoparticles."

Jimmy settled down as Bob hooked the pod back up. I stayed on the pew for the next cycle of filling and testing (now up to 94% and still non-functional) but the cross, with Christ and his rainbow coating kept drawing my attention.

Rounding the pod, and more than a little wary of being frozen by escaped vapor, I approached what was left of the altar. My emotions took me by surprise as I stood there, staring up at the wooden carving of Jesus, with his crown of thorns and the pain so effectively etched onto his face.

Not even realizing what I was doing, I dropped to my knees and put my hands together. I hadn't been to church since I was at school, didn't have a clue about prayers, so I simply said: "Please help us."

A hand touched my shoulder and I looked up to see Jimmy standing there. "You think this'll help?"

I let out a snort. "No idea. But it can't hurt, can it?"

Jimmy stared up at the cross, and the expected teasing didn't materialize. Instead he kneeled down beside me and put his hands together as well. "I thought it really strange when I first saw the pod in the middle of a church. Thought that whoever put it here had a wicked sense of humor. But I think I get it now. It's all about hope, isn't it? Hope and miracles. What better place than a church for the pod?"

I nodded, my eyes filling with tears. The rainbow was moving on as the sun rose higher. Behind us the machine said it was now 96% full and still hungry.

"Do you remember the Lord's Prayer?" Jimmy asked.

I thought hard and realized I did. The words had been ingrained by daily recitals in school. I confirmed with a nod.

"Join me then?" Jimmy asked.

As one we spoke, our voices carrying through the church: "Our Father, who art in Heaven."

"Power restarting. Diagnostics initiating. Pressure in the nanoparticle chamber is 99% and functionality is restored. Nanoparticle density is 50% and not high enough for functionality. Estimated time to recharge nanoparticles is fifteen days. Recommend recharging with MicroHealth nanoparticles. Please contact MicroHealth representative."

Sitting quietly, propped up against the wall and staring into the half closed eyes of Jesus, I didn't react at first to the machine.

"I've done it!" Bob shouted out. He sounded more surprised than I would have thought. Didn't he know what he was doing?

"It's fixed?" I joined him beside the machine. "Not the nanoparticles, at least not yet, but the nitrogen vapor issue?"

"Didn't you hear what it said?" Bob was almost jumping up and down.

Jimmy and I glanced at each other and simultaneously shook our heads.

"The pod said what it always says, didn't it?" Jimmy asked.

"How did you miss that? This is… wow." Bob hopped about, one hand on the hull.

"Can you make it repeat itself?" I pointed to the back. "Open and close the hatch."

"Yes, yes, yes!" Bob was going to have a heart attack if he didn't calm down. The scientist dashed to the rear of the pod and opened and closed the panel to the engine. "Listen," he said, and stood there, arms crossed, beaming at us.

The voice started to speak: "Power restarting. Diagnostics initiating."

No difference there.

The machine continued: "Pressure in the nanoparticle chamber is 99% and functionality is restored. Nanoparticle…"

"That's fantastic…" I was cut off by Bob.

"Shush, keep listening," he said, one hand up to silence us.

"…not high enough for functionality. Estimated time to recharge nanoparticles is fifteen days. Recommend recharging with MicroHealth nanoparticles. Please contact MicroHealth representative."

For a moment no one spoke. Then Jimmy let out a whoop and ran over to Bob. He gave him a man-squeeze then rushed at me.

"I told you it would be okay, did you hear that?" Jimmy picked me up and jigged about. "It's self-healing. Now the pressure is okay, it's growing its own nano-stuff! Fifteen days!'"

No words came to me, I couldn't quite believe the machine.

Jimmy dropped me and back-slapped Bob, the two men grinning manically. "You're going to be fixed, Kath. All better, good as new!" he yelled back at me. "Two weeks, that's it, two weeks and you'll be healthy again!"

I'd collapsed onto one of the pews and sat there staring at the machine. Cured, remission. I was beginning to love those words.

Bob separated from Jimmy and circled the machine, stroking the hull of the pod as he walked. "This is one hell of a machine. I have to know, where did it come from?"

"We actually have no idea. I was given a key to the church and told to fix myself under the agreement that I'd pass the key on to the next person."

"Does that mean…" Bob looked from me to Jimmy and then back again. "Does that mean you've got cancer?"

Not sure how a man as smart as him hadn't figured that out already, I nodded. "But things are looking much better for me after a few sessions in there."

"How better?"

"I had lots of tumors in both my lungs and my liver. Now I've only got two left. Even if the machine broke completely and you never figured out how to make enough particles to recharge the system I've got treatments open to me now that I could only dream of before." My emotions threatened to take control. I took a moment to steady myself. "The docs are talking surgery."

The pod seemed to grow and fill the room. There'd be no surgery. In two weeks from now I'd have that last session in the pod to wipe out the cancer and wouldn't have to face the needles and recovery and fresh scars driving me mad with that itch. No worry about infections or MRSA or overworked nurses. No days in the hospital wondering if one of those terrible complications I had to sign off on would happen to me. No seeing people further down the cancer path and knowing that was my future as well.

"Wow." Bob walked around to the open side of the pod. "How does it work?"

I touched the hidden panel and the lid opened. "The patient takes their shoes off and climbs in. Then when they place their hand on the panel," I pointed to the place as it came into view, "the lid closes. The machine does a scan and tells the person how many sessions it needs to fix them."

"That's it? Does it hurt? Does it use needles?"

"You know, I have no idea how it got the stuff into my system. There's no pain or injections, just feeling better afterwards."

"That's why it has to be self-charging. I bet it pumps the pod full of nanoparticles and continuously grows its own supply. Amazing." Bob was muttering again. "Have you had a go?" Bob turned to Jimmy.

Jimmy laughed. "No, mate. Not sure I'd want to."

How could he not want to? I frowned at him. Hadn't two years of watching the downside of not being diagnosed early been enough for him?

"But it's probably something I should do eventually," Jimmy added with a sheepish look.

Ah, I thought. Bigging himself up in front of the scientist.

"Fair enough." Bob touched the mattress and recoiled as it expanded around his fingers.

"The scanner still works." I crossed my arms and waited for a reaction.

Jimmy was first. "How do you know that?"

"Found out when I was here with Dad. It confirmed what the MRI said."

"Could I have a go?" Bob was already untying his shoes. He climbed in and lay there as the foam grew around him. "What now?"

I shook my head gently. Hadn't he been listening? "Put your hand up there." I pointed.

Moments later, the lid was lowering.

"Patient registered via DNA. Scan initiating." The voice spoke, as soothing and miraculous as the first time I'd heard it.

"Diagnosing."

Bob was young. I doubted it would find anything at all.

"Patient is confirmed as having fasted for minimum of eight hours. Elevated blood sugar level of 6.7 mmol/l detected. Diagnosis of prediabetes. One session required to repair pancreas."

I slid to the edge of my seat, listening. After all the cancer repairs the machine had made, and what it had found with my dad, part of me had decided this machine was for that disease only.

"Session can begin after required recharging of nanoparticles. Shall we end the session?"

Bob said yes and the lid opened. "Good thing I didn't stop for breakfast." He slapped Jimmy on the arm. "You know, I thought I was peeing a bit too much," he said with a grin. "I love this machine."

Somehow I had to get Sally out of the hospital. The machine would balance her brain chemicals or something, and she'd be fixed, happy, *normal*. Fifteen days. That's all. Just fifteen short days, I thought, and smiled.

High on the thought of curing Sally of her depression, I turned on Jimmy. "Right, your turn."

"Oh, no…" He looked sideways at the pod. "Not really interested right now."

Bob smirked as he laced up his trainers. "Afraid of the big bad machine?"

"No…" Jimmy took a cautious step towards it. "I just don't want to go in right now."

I knew this side of Jimmy, the refusal to try anything new until he was absolutely good and ready.

"Why wouldn't you want to go in right now?" I asked.

Taking a few steps towards the exit, he waved a hand dismissively. "I've got to get back to work." He checked his phone. "Got a meeting with my manager in half an hour. I've got to prepare for it."

I stifled a laugh.

Then he dropped the ultimate Jimmy avoidance line: "Some of us have to work, you know."

There would be no Jimmy scans today. I shook my head at Bob mouthing *no*. The scientist looked like he was about to start in on Jimmy in a big way. All that would do was get his back up, and I had to live with the man.

"Oh, almost forgot." The scarf lay discarded over the back of an upside down pew. My heart skipped a beat as I realized after all our precautions we'd almost walked merrily out into the street. Despite all his help in getting the machine fixed, he was still an unknown quantity to me. And to be honest, in his position, I'd make it my mission to steal the pod.

Bob complained but allowed me to wrap the scarf around his head. Jimmy opened up the car and we led him to the back seat and made him lie down again.

"Home then," I said.

The church was locked up, safe and sound. The machinery was working again, producing more of those little miracle particles. A plan to break Sally out of the hospital was hatching in my brain. I'd get her here in fifteen days on the nose and mend her broken brain. She'd be the Sally of old, before she started showing symptoms. I blew a kiss to the giant oak door as Jimmy pulled away.

Despite being blindfolded and tossed in the backseat of our car, Bob chattered non-stop all the way home. He was spewing all kinds of technical talk that I didn't understand a word of. I think he was a step further down the line to figuring out the nanoparticles we'd given him. Maybe he'd memorized enough of the guts of the machine to start making his own. That would be fine with me. Then he wouldn't have to steal ours.

I stretched back, feeling a little more comfortable, more rested and secure than I had in some time. A slight smile on Jimmy's lips was probably matched with my own version. This was the time to be quietly confident, if ever there was one.

Home was as we left it, with Bob's old Fiesta like a stain on the pavement. If he did figure out the secrets of the machine he'd soon have more money than he'd know what to do with. I wondered if he'd keep Bessie.

I opened up the front door. Bob was emerging from the backseat, the scarf now in his hands and still babbling scientific nonsense at us. The postie had been and I picked up the letters, shuffling though as I made my way to the kitchen. The day had started early and I was desperate for a decent cup of tea.

Halfway to the kitchen I stopped dead. There among the bills and junk mail was a creamy envelope with my name handwritten in tidy script. I dropped the other cards on the table and ripped the flap.

That Elusive Cure

"Oh my god, oh my god, oh my god."

Jimmy came up behind me and peered over my shoulder. "What is it?"

"It's from Richard Newland."

He shook his head, confused. "Who?"

"Newland, he's the guy that started all of this. He's the guy who owns the church."

"Oh shit." Jimmy sat heavily on a chair. "What did you ask him?"

I put a hand to my tummy to try and quell the growing butterflies there. "I don't remember exactly. Just asked where the machine came from, I think." I scanned the letter, too anxious to read it word for word. I saw something about trips away and...

"Oh no."

"What? What is it?" Jimmy sat forward, his eyes fixed on the letter. "What does he say?"

Aware of Bob standing somewhere behind me, and unsure whether he should be privy to the letter, I read the letter out regardless.

Here goes nothing, I thought and began to speak.

"Dear Kath,

Thank you for your letter. I must admit it was a great surprise to be found. I was under the impression that my part in this was anonymous."

That was funny, it seemed Mr. Newland was like an urban legend when it came to the machine, with his name bandied about by all and sundry.

"It has been a number of years since I last set eyes on the church and that wonderful MicroHealth pod. I would very much like to see it again."

Shit, shit, shit. The words blurred as I tried to see the entire letter all at the same time.

"I do hope that wonderful machine has given you a new lease of life – a cancer-free life as it has surely done to so many people already. I'm not sure I can answer as many questions as you hope about the origins, but I will certainly do my best.

The health benefit from the machine means I have retained the energy levels of a far younger man. Although I'm in my eighties now, I still hold the reins to my company. I have to attend a business gathering in Scotland next week, after that I would be honored to meet you and see the machine one more time."

If I could push him back enough the pod might have finished fixing itself. Maybe, just maybe we'd get through this without anyone realizing we'd broken the precious machine.

"I feel the time has come to confess how I came to own the machine, and I look forward to imparting this knowledge on you. I will call closer to the date of my visit.

Warm regards,
Rich"

Jimmy stared at me, a stunned expression on his face. I figured mine matched.

"I need to be there. You can say I'm your brother."

I'd forgotten about Bob.

The scientist continued, "If I know how it was made maybe I can find out more about how the machinery works and move towards manufacturing more pods. Imagine having one in every hospital." He paused then said, "There wouldn't be hospitals anymore, they'd be in every doctor's office. No sick people anymore." His eyes glazed over. "We'll be the richest people on the planet."

Jimmy looked over my shoulder at Bob, the mention of money grabbing his attention.

"Look you two, before you decide what color your Lamborghini is going to be let's get through this meeting with Rich. Okay?"

I stalked through to the kitchen and up to the calendar. In black marker I wrote 15 on today's square and circled it. Then I wrote 14 on tomorrow's and kept going until I got to the number 1. On the Tuesday two weeks and a day away I drew an X. Nerves got the better of me again, and I capped the pen and dropped it back into the pen pot, wondering how on earth I would last the fortnight.

TWENTY-SEVEN

Losing It

Thursday arrived and I woke up with the knowledge that at about ten o'clock a bunch of consultants and doctors would all be in a meeting room discussing my case. Dr. Whoever-he-was who had subbed for our regular oncologist last week had mentioned surgery, and I still couldn't believe it. Even if the pod never worked again I had new options open to me.

Jimmy came into the bedroom with two cups of tea. "Good morning. Do you remember what's happening today?"

He put one of the mugs on my bedside cabinet and stood by the door while I plumped my pillows and sat up.

"Yes, of course I remember. It's the MDT."

"When I spoke to Mr. Noble's nurse Jill she said she'd phone afterwards. Expect the phone to ring after midday. Excited?"

Still waking up, I wasn't sure what I was feeling. I certainly wasn't as anxious as I should have been. But that's because in a mere twelve days whatever the doctors came up with wouldn't matter anymore. I'd be cured and their proposed treatment would be moot.

"I might go out and ignore it all," I said watching Jimmy for a reaction. "I got me a loverboy over at the gym. He texted me and maybe I'll pay him a visit."

Jimmy snorted. "You haven't been to the gym in two years."

I tried not to laugh. "Maybe I started going and didn't tell you."

"That reminds me. Do you know we're still paying for your membership? Seems a waste. Could spend that money in better ways."

"But how will I see my loverboy?"

Jimmy left, chuckling as he went into his study.

I lay there a while, sipping my tea and imagining a meeting room deep inside one of the Aintree hospital buildings, an unknown number of doctors and consultants giving my file time, studying my scans, deciding on my future. Jill would phone once she had news, but that wouldn't be until the afternoon if past experience was anything to go by.

The book I'd been reading didn't appeal. I did try, but the third time I read the same page and still didn't absorb the words I gave up. A shower helped. I stood under the water, the temperature as hot as I could stand until my skin hurt and my head cleared. No point fretting. The machine would indeed finish recharging itself and I'd have no need for whatever the doctors were planning.

The phone rang as I dressed. I ran for it, my heart beating hard. Midday was a bit early, but maybe I was first on the list. I grabbed the handset and answered it breathlessly.

"Yes?"

"Mum, it's me." Cass, not the nurse, and she sounded like she was crying.

"What's wrong?"

"It's the baby, Mum. I'm losing it." She burst into tears.

"Oh no, Cass. Is Jack with you?"

Through her sobs I made out a yes.

"Sweetheart, I'm coming over." I struggled with my socks one-handed. "I'll be over in half an hour. You hold on."

I hung up and rushed the last of my clothes on.

"Jimmy, I've got to go to Cass's. She's losing the baby."

Jimmy looked up from his computer. "Well, maybe that's for the best. They are so young."

"Jesus, Jimmy. Have a heart why don't you." I shot him a dirty look.

"Hey, just saying. It's sad, but these things happen."

Men. I turned and stalked off, grabbing my keys and leaving without so much as a goodbye. Jesus, how could he be so cold?

How far had things gone with Cass? Maybe the machine had charged up faster than anticipated. If the baby was still alive in her, maybe it could fix things. I veered off the route to Cass's flat and stopped at the church. Since the fiasco with Jimmy I kept the key with me at all times. I opened up and ran inside. The panel opened and closed smoothly and the machine spoke the words that were now so familiar to me.

"Power restarting. Diagnostics initiating. Pressure in the nanoparticle chamber is 99% and functionality is restored. Nanoparticle density is 60% and not high enough for functionality. Estimated time to recharge nanoparticles is twelve days. Recommend recharging with MicroHealth nanoparticles. Please contact MicroHealth representative."

I slammed my hand into the nearest pew. Shit. "Why can't you be fixed?" I shouted at the pod.

Cass was waiting for me, and this stupid machine was useless. I locked up and drove too fast to my daughter's flat. If only I hadn't hidden the key at home. If only Jimmy hadn't *had* to look inside the machinery. If only he hadn't broken the damn pipe. I'd be fixed and I could race Cass over and mend the little baby inside of her. Tears welled up at the unfairness of it all.

I found Cass in a huddle on her bed. Jack attended her, playing a far better nurse to her than I could right now. The doctor had already paid them a visit, the advice given to let nature take its course. Feeling impotent I sat with her, listening to her cry and holding her hand.

As late afternoon drew in, Jack suggested I go. His usual Goth makeup was absent and he looked ten years younger, like nothing more than a child playing at adults. I gave them both hugs and let them have their privacy.

The drive home was slower than the panicked race over earlier. But a deep anger was growing in me, anger at Jimmy for messing up, for breaking a miracle machine. I pulled in the driveway as a rage descended on me.

Slamming the front door as I came in, I shouted up the stairs, "Jimmy get down here now!"

"What's wrong with you?" He appeared on the half landing looking unsure.

"Your daughter is miscarrying your first grandchild and your reaction was a shrug of the shoulders. How can you be so fucking cold?"

He started at my words. "Just because I don't break down in tears doesn't mean I don't feel. How dare you." He turned to go back upstairs.

"Oh no you don't. Get down here."

He hesitated.

"Now!" I shrieked and lobbed my keys at him. "Cass's baby has died and I could have fucking fixed it! If you hadn't broken the machine, if you hadn't been such a fucking meddler, then none of this would be happening!"

Jimmy recoiled, rubbing his arm where the keys hit. "I don't have to listen to this. I'll talk to you when you're rational."

"Don't you fucking 'rational' me." I took the stairs two at a time, chasing him down. He'd gone to hide in his study. I grabbed a file off the shelf and heaved it at him. "You fucked it all up! I could have been cancer-free by now. Cass could be fine, but no, you had to have a look. You had to have a fiddle. Couldn't you have kept your big clumsy fucking fingers to yourself?"

He sat there silently, his expression dark.

"What if you hadn't found Bob? Then what? You wouldn't have a clue what to do. The machine wouldn't have stood a fucking chance with you ballsing it up."

I grabbed a pencil pot and hit him in the chest with it. Pens and pencils flew in all directions.

"You're an idiot, you know that, a fucking idiot!"

Jimmy remained infuriatingly silent.

"Answer me!" I stepped towards him, and he flinched. "I'm not going to hit you, for god's sake, I just want an answer. Why did you have to break my miracle?"

That was it. The tears started to flow. I stood there, weeping, feeling the sadness that seemed to root itself deep in my soul. Jimmy did nothing, just sat there, fingers linked across his belly, his eyes narrowed into slits.

"Dad's got prostate cancer. The machine diagnosed him," I said between sobs. "What if it never works again and he dies?"

Jimmy didn't move.

"Goddamn it, don't you have any emotions?" I was reaching for another folder when the phone rang.

"You going to get that?" Jimmy finally spoke, his voice cold.

Wiping my eyes and dragging in steadying breaths I picked up the handset.

"Hello, may I speak to Kath Wyatt?"

"This is Kath," I replied.

"Oh hi, Kath. It's Jill here. I have news."

I wiped at my face, trying to dry the tears while the nurse spoke.

"Mr. Wright doesn't feel he could successfully remove all the tumors. One of them is very close to the hepatic artery and he's not convinced he'd be able to get clear margins."

I slumped against the wall.

Jill continued, "There was a specialist in radiotherapy in the room when your case was being discussed. Dr. Feldman says you're an ideal candidate for a new kind of treatment called radioembolisation or SIRTs. His nurse will be in contact shortly to make an appointment with you."

I thanked her for calling and hung up the phone. Not the news I'd expected. I couldn't deal with anymore changes and went to lie down. The bedroom was cold and I threw the covers over me and hugged a pillow. The rage had dissipated but the harm had been done. No matter how much Jimmy deserved my anger it didn't help matters. Tears flowed again, and I pulled my legs close and cried myself to sleep.

TWENTY-EIGHT

Dreaming of a Great Escape

Dear Sally,

I wonder when they'll let me call you. Hopefully the nurses and doctors are treating you right and you're getting the treatment you need. When do you think they'll let you out for a day? The weather has been fabulous. We need to go down to New Brighton with the kids. You and I can lie on towels while the two of them build sandcastles and play in the sea.

There's one of those pirate re-enactments they do at Fort Perch in a couple of weekends. I thought Wendy might let me take the kids there, that is if they haven't let you out by then. I could make them pirate clothes and color Peter's face so it looks like he's got stubble. Which one of them should I give an eye patch to? Remember all the costumes I made for Cass when she was little? You were always amazed at them. I might have some of the better ones in the attic still. Maybe I should get them down for the kids?

If the docs don't let you out for an entire day, maybe they'll let me take you to the park? We could go to Royden park and walk around watching the dogs and debating which one we liked best.

I'm thinking of you all the time, Sal. Hurry up and come home.

Kath xxxoooxxx

I reread the letter and decided I'd put just enough hints at taking her off safely for a day. The machine would only need ten minutes to do its thing, once it had recharged and was working again. She needed to last out another eleven days. That wasn't so much.

Sealing up the letter, I decided once again to drive to the hospital. Most of the journey was on the motorway and driving fast suited me right now. I blasted the music but didn't really listen what was playing and put my foot down far too heavily.

Jimmy flitted in and out of mind as I drove. He'd not spoken to me since my outburst yesterday and I wasn't about to apologize for being angry at something he'd done wrong. We'd survived cancer where so many other couples can't cope with the stress, and a strange machine from the future – if that's what it was – is what does us in. The bed felt so big during the night, like a chasm had opened up between us. I'd give it another day then try talking to him. Today I was too wound up with thoughts of Sally to deal with him as well.

I concentrated on the road and tried to shake myself free of angry thoughts. Just in case I could go in to see her I needed to be calm and open to her needs, not hung up on my own issues. But I couldn't help but think that I could have had her in the machine and well before the breakdown had even happened.

That Elusive Cure

A road sign flashed past. Another half hour to go, roughly, before I got there. Someone else was travelling, Rich Newland. Next week he was coming to see the machine. My heart jumped at the thought. Somehow I had to put him off for a week, let the pod finish recharging. If I told him we were going on holiday that might work, but then again, if I were him, I'd have a second key. I pictured the big old-fashioned design in my mind and wondered if they could even be copied. Everyone had those Yale type keys these days. I'd go down to the shop in Moreton later and see what the man could do about making a duplicate.

The other thing I wanted to do was nip down to the church and check on the progress of the machine, make sure it was recharging on schedule. Lots could happen with nearly two weeks until it was supposed to be working again. Who knows, maybe they'd release Sally before the machine had finished growing its nanoparticles and I could take her to the church without stealing her. Would tinkering with her brain change her? Maybe she'd come out of the pod with a different personality? How much of her and the way she behaved was down to being bipolar?

Finally the turn off for the hospital appeared and I veered off onto country roads. Just over an hour after leaving home, I parked at the hospital. Grabbing my letter I walked into the reception and got the attention of a nurse.

"It's for Sally Jones," I said as he accepted my letter. "How is she doing?"

The nurse gave me a professional blank stare. "We can only give information to her sister."

"Am I able to visit her yet?" I leaned up against the counter.

"Sorry, but she's not ready for that."

"But I just want to see her for a moment."

He crossed his arms. "I can't allow that."

"Can you pass messages between us?"

"I'm sorry but the only contact can be with relatives."

I took a deep breath, my temper was still on quick boil. "But I've known Sally since we were four. I've seen more of her than anyone on this planet. Surely you can tell me *something*?"

"I'm sorry. Only relatives."

"Would you give me a letter if she wrote one back?"

"In theory, yes."

In theory. What a load of tosh. Frustrated I left and started the long drive home, but not after staring for ages at the windows and wondering if Sally was behind one of them, staring back at me.

TWENTY-NINE

Party Planning

First thing I did Saturday morning was dash over to the church and test the pod. The result was what I expected, but not what I hoped for. Ten days to go. What I wanted was a miraculous jump in production, and to have the machine say it was one day away from working, or even two.

I'd made Jimmy a cup of tea earlier and said a good morning. Sometimes the two of us were so stubborn the best thing to do was move past an issue, not apportion blame. I'd seen the look in his eye when he thought I wasn't paying attention. He felt guilty for buggering up the machine, very guilty. And I had to admit, if it wasn't for him getting in contact with Bob, we'd never have got to this point. We'd still have a broken machine and no clue how to fix it.

Dad had called a secret meeting with Margret down at the boat yard. We were going to be holding the meeting at a café nearby. I think the idea was to drink tea and plan the party Mum supposedly didn't know anything about. To be honest, making small talk with a woman I knew nothing about didn't appeal to me, especially today. Between Jimmy, Margret, Sally, the pod and so many other things that were going wrong right now, I was getting pretty stressed. There was no reason to think that the machine wouldn't fix itself, yet it was all I could think about, central to everything I worried about.

"Hi Dad," I said as I rounded the side of a building and caught him standing by his boat with that woman beside him. The two of them stood too close together for my liking, with her hand resting on his shoulder and him looking intensely at her. For a moment my guts went cold, had I been blind to an actual affair? Then Margret turned to me. She seemed to be sad. Surprised at being caught in the act of trying to steal my dad more like. Maybe that's what her guilty expression looked like.

"Kathy, how lovely to see you again." She gave me a hug despite me trying to avoid contact, and as she pulled back I realized she was crying.

"What's wrong?" I pulled a tissue from my pocket and handed it to her. Dad stood close beside her. Dad looked watery-eyed as well.

Margret steadied herself. "I knew what was going on with you and your health, so I didn't tell your father. I figured there was enough worry going on there."

I glanced at Dad, hoping for a clue. But he was staring at the ground sadly.

"It's my husband, you see. He was diagnosed with cancer six months ago. He died last night." She burst into tears again.

"She didn't want to worry us, not when we had you to worry about," Dad told me quietly, his voice almost lost on the sea wind. He was still staring at the ground, one arm placed awkwardly around Margret's shoulders.

"Jesus, how awful." I gave Margret another hug. "Please accept my condolences."

"I'm sorry, so sorry," she said as she dried her eyes. The tears had gone again and she dabbed her cheeks dry as she attempted to compose herself.

"What on earth are you apologizing for?" I took out the travel pack of tissues from my pocket, thought about giving her another one, then handed her the pack. "Can I take you home? Or is there somewhere else you'd like to be?"

Margret gazed out towards the tidal islands. "Mark loved walking to Hilbre Island. If you don't mind, I'd like to walk out there."

The tides were in our favor and Dad and I walked Margret out past Little Eye and Middle Island to the biggest of the three islands. Margret walked to the far end and sat on a grassy mound, watching the colony of seals as they chattered and readied themselves to go out to sea for the day. Dad and I sat close, both of us unsure about how close to sit and what to say.

The sun moved up to its apex as more walkers appeared. The tides would turn soon and trap us on the island. If Margret didn't make a start I'd have to interrupt her thoughts, but before I had to she stood and without a word turned to leave.

Death did funny things to people. I'd told Cass I'd come by hers after party planning. As we walked back along the beach I felt like I was surrounded by death and dying, if not of other people, then of myself.

We took Margret back home and made a move to leave only because she insisted. A dog I didn't know she owned walked stiffly out of a back room and sat next to her before starting to lick her hand.

"Mark's dog," she said and patted him on the head. "He's not far off joining his master."

"Do you want me to fix you anything?"

Dad stood by the door fiddling with the rim of his hat. He looked so uncomfortable, I'd have sent him away to wait outside but I was certain he'd refuse.

"I could make you a cup of tea? Are you hungry?" I moved to sit next to Margret on the sofa.

"Buster has cancer as well. Seems that dreadful disease is everywhere I look."

A shape distended the dog's belly. I saw it now I was sitting down. Did the machine cure animals as well? What would happen if I put Buster in the pod? Surely it couldn't make things any worse for him? All the dog had to look forward to was waiting until Margret had the courage to put him down. Seemed my list of possible patients was growing ever longer by the day.

"If you need help with Buster, you know, as you make arrangements for Mark, I'd be happy to babysit him for you."

Margret put a hand on my knee. "You're such a lovely girl." She smiled at me, her expression bittersweet. "Don't worry about me, I'll be okay."

I put my number on a pad by the phone and told her to call me, no matter the time, if she needed anything. We embraced, Dad giving her another of those shoulder hugs he always did when he felt uncomfortable.

"I had no idea she even had a husband," he said once we were back in my car.

"Some people don't like to make a fuss, do they? They just want to get on with life and try to feel as normal as possible." I thought of me and my battle with that horrible disease. I'd gone underground, quit work, barely left the house, stopped talking to all but a few of my friends. Everyone coped in the best way for them.

THIRTY

Newland Phones

"Fuck."

Jimmy put the phone down as I walked into the house. I'd been with Cass all morning, helping out around her flat as she recovered. "What's wrong?"

"Newland."

One word, but enough to scare me into dropping my handbag on the hall floor.

"What about him?" I asked quietly.

"He's coming tomorrow, leaving early in the morning." He punched the wall. "Fuck."

I grabbed my bag and took the church key from it. "It's too early, the pod isn't ready yet." I waved the key at him, as if it made more of a point. "You should have delayed him somehow."

"You think I didn't try? This is a man used to getting his own way. There was nothing I said that put him off. Nothing at all."

"Shit, shit, shit." I sat on the stairs and fiddled with the key. "What are we going to do?"

Jimmy was rubbing his knuckles. "Lie. Tell him someone before us did it. Or we could tell the truth. Those are the choices as I see it."

Which was worse, the lie or the truth? I wasn't sure. "I'm going to the church. Maybe it charged up faster."

"You've gone just about every day. Is it charging faster?"

"No, but I'm going to do it anyway. You coming or staying?"

Jimmy checked his phone. "I've got to be back by two o'clock for a meeting. Come on, let's go."

He drove, weaving in and out of traffic recklessly. Guess it wasn't just me whose nerves were getting the better of them. Jimmy screeched to a halt outside the church and seconds later we were inside.

"Open it then," I said nodding towards the back of the pod.

"No way. I'm never touching that thing again."

Maybe the man did learn lessons. I opened and closed the hatch and the machine went through its diagnostics. Seven days left until the recharge was complete. Right on schedule. I heard a noise and looked over to see Jimmy grimacing and holding his right hand gingerly.

"What have you done?" I went to him and checked his hand. The knuckles were already turning shades of blue and purple.

"Punched it, didn't I." I glanced at the pew.

"Silly man." I leaned over and gently kissed his hand.

"Where do you think it came from?" He indicated at the pod.

I shook my head. "I have no idea. Space? Aliens? The future?"

"Why do you always assume it's from the future?"

That made me turn away from the pod and look curiously at Jimmy. "What do you mean?"

He walked up to it, tentatively reaching out to touch the silver hull. "Do you really think time travel will ever be possible?" He raised his eyebrows at me. "Think about it. If it was possible wouldn't we have people flying back and forth from the future to the present? Well they don't, I can assure you."

"How would you have any idea whether people time travel? They could be fixing things, doing things like leaving this machine here."

"And risk changing the future? They could cause a paradox and never exist and we'd be caught in a time loop, repeating forever."

I snorted at what sounded like science fiction.

"I'm being serious. Think about the earthquake in Japan. That destroyed a nuclear power plant, didn't it? Now the Pacific Ocean is being poisoned by the radioactivity pouring from the mess that was left. Don't you think if time travel was possible someone would have come back to fix that?"

This was making my head hurt. I put my hand up to stop him. "Okay, let's assume time travel is out. Why not aliens?"

"The pod speaks in English."

"Could be a babel fish effect," I shot back at him. "If it's alien and advanced enough to fix us, surely it would be advanced enough to be able to speak to different species." I thought of Buster. If I put him inside would it bark at him?

"Fair enough, but then it wouldn't have *MicroHealth* written inside the lid." He crossed his arms as if to drive home his point, flinching when his injured right hand touched his left arm.

I shrugged. "Okay. But if you've eliminated aliens and the future, what's left?"

Jimmy circled the pod, a cryptic expression on his face.

"Everyone hates a know-it-all, Jimmy," I said. "And even worse is a know-it-all who doesn't spill."

"Once you eliminate the impossible, whatever remains, no matter how improbable, must be the truth." He stopped and made a point of smirking at me.

"So what remains?" I was losing patience.

"That the machine is from the present. That someone, somewhere on this planet invented this machine some time ago and this beauty is the result."

Could Jimmy be right? Was someone out there making these things for a select few and keeping the rest of the world's population in the dark? "Bloody hell," I said and sat heavily on a pew.

"Mind-blowing thought, isn't it?"

"Do you think it's been stolen from somewhere?" My fingers twisted up together as I tried to work out what this would mean. "What if the owner isn't Rich and they want it back? Maybe that's the reason for the secrecy and why only one person can use it at a time? Wouldn't want the numbers of cured people to be noticeable, right?"

Jimmy held his hands up. "I'm just doing what I do. I'm an analyst. I analyzed the possibilities. Besides,

Newland will be here tomorrow and he's planning on telling us where the machine came from, right?"

"I guess. He did say that in the letter." The pod seemed too fantastical not to be from the future.

"Then assuming he forgives us for breaking-"

"And don't forget fixing," I interrupted.

"And fixing his wonderful machine, then we will soon know the truth."

My phone vibrated inside my handbag, breaking the moment. I dug inside for it.

"Damn it, it's Janie again."

The phone displayed her message. *Haven't heard back from you. Hope everything is okay and life is treating you alright. If you have a minute I'd love to hear how the machine has changed things for you.*

I could feel the hurt emanating from her words. She didn't deserve to be ignored. "Maybe I should tell her what happened? Admit the truth to her."

"When's the machine going to be fixed?"

"Next Tuesday," I said as I stared at her message.

"Tell her you'll meet her next Wednesday. All being well, you'll be fixed by then and you won't have to lie to her."

Got a busy week. Want to meet at the café in Thurstaton you took me to next Wednesday? I'd love to see you again.

The message came back quickly. *Would love to. I'll be there at 1. We can have lunch.*

I put the phone back in my handbag and stared at the pod. It had better be fixed on time.

THIRTY-ONE

A Plane Crash

All Wednesday morning I waited at home, listening for the phone. Newland had told Jimmy he was leaving early. How long did it take to fly down from Scotland? I suppose it depended on where in Scotland he was. I reckoned from Glasgow or Edinburgh to Liverpool Airport couldn't be more than an hour. From further north it wouldn't add that much time. Hell, I could drive there in a day.

Jimmy said Newland told him to expect a call around lunchtime. The clock told me midday had come and gone by half an hour. What was lunchtime for Newland?

I checked the house again and saw a piece of fluff on the carpet. The curtains needed straightening in their pullbacks, even though I must have done that at least twice before. The hall cupboard needed tidying. I was down on my knees sorting through shoes when I heard Jimmy calling from upstairs.

"Kath, you've got to come and see this." There was urgency to his tone that I didn't like.

Just in case it was while I was upstairs that Newland decided not to phone but show up on the door instead, I shoved the shoes back in and closed the door.

I joined Jimmy in his study. He'd been taking a break from work and one of his regular news sites was up on the screen. There was a picture of a smiling white-haired man. Underneath a red banner said *Breaking News*.

"What is it?" I pulled up the spare chair and sat beside him.

"Read the headline."

CEO believed among the dead as three bodies are pulled from plane crash in Liverpool.

I clicked on the picture of the elderly man, muttering, "Oh shit," as I did so.

Three people were killed when a private jet overshot the runway at Liverpool John Lennon Airport earlier today. An airport spokesman said two crew and one passenger were on board the Gulfstream 450 when it skidded off the runway in heavy rain as the pilot attempted to land at 10:14am this morning.

Richard Newland, reclusive billionaire and founder of the MicroHealth medical technology company has been confirmed as among the dead.

"There are no known survivors," the spokesman said.

A representative from the North West Ambulance Service confirmed that the five attending ambulance crews had been stood down. No one was taken to hospital following the crash.

Fire crews based at the airport reached the blazing jet within two minutes of the crash, airport officials said.

JLA is expected to remain closed for some time, with incoming flights being diverted to Manchester. Passengers expecting to fly from Liverpool this afternoon are urged to contact their airline.

Early eye-witness accounts describe black smoke billowing from the burnt out fuselage.

I sat back, my hands dropping into my lap. "Oh shit."

"Guess we'll never know the secrets of the pod now," Jimmy said as he scanned for more news articles on the crash.

I hit him on the arm. "A man is dead, in fact three people are dead, and that's all you can think about?"

"What? We didn't know the man. A month ago neither of us would have even noticed the news of this crash."

I felt a weight of responsibility forming on my shoulders. With the owner of the pod dead, someone had to keep an eye on the machine and the church. I decided that person would have to be me. I'd have to find out what was going to happen to the ownership of the building. If needs be, we'd have to move the pod before the church was put up for sale or handed to some unknowing relative. Newland wasn't young, hopefully he'd made provisions for the church in his will.

Jimmy found another article about the crash. I scanned it, searching for more information. With this Newland owning a company called MicroHealth, it became pretty certain where and when the pod came from. I hated it when Jimmy was right.

THIRTY-TWO

An Overdose

The phone rang four times before I picked up. What if investigators into Newland's death suspected foul play and they found my number in his recent calls list? Could they work that fast? I answered with a cautious, "Hello?"

"May I speak with Kathy Wyatt, please."

Oh God, they *had* connected me to Newland.

"Speaking..." An urge to slam the phone down came over me. Somehow I resisted.

"Oh, hello Kathy. It's Wendy here."

Wendy? It took me a second to realize who she was. "Hi, you're calling about Sally. Is there any news?"

"That's why I'm phoning. I've got a number for you. You can contact her now."

I sagged against the wall. "Thank God. I was beginning to worry they'd never let me speak to her. How is she doing?"

"As well as can be expected. She's had a rough couple of weeks." Wendy recited the number for me and rang off. I admitted I was surprised she'd kept up her part of the deal and given me a contact number. I'd spent so many years hating Wendy alongside Sally that it was weird to be in league with her.

I dialed the number, feeling my excitement growing. We could plan to take her out for the day. I could get her down to the pod and fix her dodgy head. Only five days to go and the machine would be functional. Such a small number of days. A big grin spread across my face.

Finally the phone was answered.

"Hello, can I speak to Sally Jones. I'm Kathy Wyatt. I believe she's been given permission to talk to me."

A female voice told me, "I'll see about finding her. I'm just going to put you on hold for a moment."

No music to ease the wait with this system, just a quiet static hum to give me a clue I was still connected to the hospital. No one came back to me for a long time, and I was on the verge of hanging up when there was the sound of the line reconnecting and someone manhandling a handset.

"Hello?" A man this time.

"Hi, I've been on hold for a while. A woman was looking for Sally Jones for me."

"Right, I'll see what I can do."

"Wait-"

He put me on hold before I could ask how long he might be. I sat on the stool by the phone and tapped on my knee while the static played into my ear.

"Hello?" A woman again. I wasn't sure if it was the first person again or another woman.

"Hi, this is Kathy Wyatt. Was it you I spoke to before? You were looking for Sally Jones for me. She's a patient."

"Ah, yes, that was my colleague. Who is it you're looking for again?"

"Sally Jones," I said, trying to mask my frustration. "I think there are two people searching for her now."

"Yes, well, let me find out what's going on."

Jesus. Was it that hard to find patients? What kind of place were they running?

The phone crackled in my ear again. "Hello, are you looking for Sally Jones?" Could be the second woman was back on the line.

I sighed. "Yes, I am."

"What is your name again?"

"Kathy Wyatt."

"You're not on the list." There was the sound of papers rustling.

"I should be, her sister Wendy gave me the number and told me to call."

"Yes, that's right. But there's been an incident. Sally can't come to the phone right now."

I sat up. "What do you mean?"

"Well, I can't tell you. That's what I meant. Only her sister Wendy Theodore is on the list. I am not allowed to divulge information to anyone else."

"Is she okay? Can you tell me anything?"

"Sorry. You'll have to call her sister."

"Thanks, will do." I hung up and got a dial tone again, saying, "Shit," over and over as I plugged in the number for Wendy's mobile.

"Wendy," I said as she picked up. "Something's wrong with Sally. They wouldn't let me talk to her.

All they'd tell me was there's been an incident." I paced the hall holding the handset with both hands.

"Calm down and explain this to me slowly."

I did so, relating my trouble getting through.

"Stay where you are. I'll ring the hospital now and find out what's going on."

I could hear the worry in her voice as she said her goodbyes. With a history of suicide in the family, I had to admit that my lovely Sally being dead was the first thing that came to mind.

Wendy took a long time coming back to me. I fixed a cup of tea and sat beside the phone, waiting for almost an hour before it finally rang. I snatched up the handset.

"Hello?"

"It's me again, Wendy."

"What's happened to her, what's wrong with Sally?"

"I'm on my way to her now. They've taken her to hospital, she's gone to Arrowe Park. She attempted suicide."

"Oh shit." Somehow I kept hold of the handset as bottom of my stomach seemed to collapse inside me.

"I'll know more when I get there."

"You'll phone me as soon as you know anything?"

"Of course I will. I'm going to list you as family as well, so you'll be able to find out information for yourself. You'll be listed as her sister."

Suddenly I felt so awful for bad-talking her with Sal all these years. "Thank you, Wendy."

"I've got to go. I'm in the car and the last thing I need is a ticket or worse to crash on the way."

That Elusive Cure

"Yes, of course. Wendy, you've no idea what it means to have you list me as family."

"Why don't you meet me over here? Give me a ring once you've arrived."

We ended the phone call, and I suddenly felt so lost. Everything was happening too fast. The machine wasn't fixed yet, I couldn't do anything to help Sal. It was all so unfair.

Wendy met me in the lobby area at the front of the hospital. She approached looking grey with worry and indicated that we sit on one of the bench seats just behind the large circular welcome desk.

"I thought before you saw her I should warn you what's going on."

I nodded, terrified of what I was about to hear.

"They think Sally got a hold of around forty Paracetamol tablets and took them either yesterday morning or Wednesday evening. The first they knew anything was wrong was when she started vomiting. They put it down to a virus and sent her to bed. The doctor looked her over, but apparently it's really difficult to diagnose Paracetamol overdose in the first day or two."

"So how is she now, did they pump her stomach?"

Wendy shook her head. "It was too late for that. They've got her on a drip with a drug that's supposed to counteract the Paracetamol, but it's only really effective in the first few hours."

"So what else are they going to do?"

Wendy looked like she might be about to cry. I reached out and took her hands between my own.

"Nothing," she finally said. "It's up to her whether she survives or not."

"What do you mean, nothing?"

Wendy waited while a surge of chattering people came through the lobby. The place emptied enough for her to be heard again, and she continued, "The damage to her liver is already done. All we can hope is that she's one of the few who makes it through. The doctor said if she makes it to day five, then chances are she'll live."

I sat back, stunned by what Wendy said. "Surely there's something else they can do?"

Wendy shook her head.

"But… waiting? That's it? We just have to wait and see?"

"Once the damage is done all they can do is keep her alive and hope she heals."

"Jesus."

"She's waiting for you," Wendy said as she dabbed her eyes with a tissue.

I drew in a deep breath, wondering how I'd cope. Sally wouldn't be pleased with me if I broke down at her bedside. I needed to put my strong face on. Wendy led me down the main corridor to the lifts and then up to the second floor where the High Dependency Unit was located.

"Prepare yourself. She seems very… different."

Deciding not to question Wendy on what she meant, I followed her to a room where there were three beds. Sally was in the middle one. There was some kind of air mattress under her and it seemed to swallow her up. Sally was only tiny, but she seemed even smaller now. She caught my attention with a weak smile, her eyes wide and adding to her child-like appearance.

Sal raised her hand and I sat next to her, taking her hand, surprised at how cold her fingers were.

"Oh, you silly woman. How did you end up here?"

Sally shrugged, a tiny movement that I barely noticed. "I'm so sorry," she said, her voice a mere breath with faint words.

"No, don't you dare apologize."

From what Wendy told me as we walked through the hospital corridors, I knew Sally's liver was failing. I'd seen enough medical dramas on the telly to know what to look out for, and although her skin was merely pale, I still wasn't prepared for the horrible mustardy yellow of her eyes. The lovely healthy whites were gone, her blue irises standing out in the sickly shade.

Wendy leaned over and placed a gentle kiss on her sister's forehead. "Is it okay if I go find something to eat, Sally? It'll give you two a chance to talk."

Sally nodded, again, the movement barely perceptible.

I stroked Sally's hand and watched as Wendy left the room. There were two other beds in the room, one was empty and the other had an elderly woman hooked up to all kinds of machines. A mask on her face wheezed out oxygen every time she inhaled. A bag with what I assumed was urine was hooked up to the bottom of her bed, a tube disappearing under the sheets. Two drips fed into her, one on either side. As far as I could tell, the woman was unconscious. Was that how Sally would end up in a couple of days' time? Wendy said her organs would start failing one by one until eventually life could no longer be sustained.

The worst of it was I could have stopped all this. If only the machine hadn't been broken. If I'd thought of taking her there right at the beginning. If Sal had taken her overdose five days later, giving the machine a chance to start working again. Then I could steal her from the hospital and fix her forever. So many ifs. I brushed aside a tear and tried to smile for Sally.

"Hey chick. Can I do anything for you?"

"It hurts," Sally said, and hovered her other hand above her liver. "It hurts all the time, no matter what they give me for the pain."

"Are they treating you right, I've heard…" I didn't have the courage to finish my thought. But as always, Sal knew what I meant.

"Because I attempted suicide, you think they'd treat me badly? Well don't worry. They're being lovely."

The nurses were off in their station just beyond the door to Sal's room. I could hear their quiet chatter. The other patient in the room still seemed to be out for the count. Leaning in close, I spoke in a whisper. "I need to break you out of here, I can mend you."

Sal managed to laugh. "And how do you think you're going to do that?"

"You noticed how well I looked before you went into the psych ward. There's a reason. I've been using a machine that fixes people. You get in and it figures out what's wrong. I'm almost cancer-free."

Sal laughed again. "And they say I'm the crazy one."

"I'm being serious. You need to hang on for a few days, it's broken right now. But it'll be fixed in four days. Then I can make you better."

"Kath, you know you sound totally bonkers, right?"

I did. I sounded insane. What if Sal said something, and they thought she was having another psychotic break? "You're right. It would be wonderful, though, wouldn't it? A machine that fixed everything? No more needles, no more medicines. Just lie down and zap, you're mended."

"I'm very tired now." Sal closed her eyes. "I do like the sound of your machine. You should get someone to invent it." She chuckled quietly.

I sat there, holding her hand and staring out the window at the park beyond the hospital as Sal's breathing settled into a sleeping rhythm. Occasionally she'd squirm a little and moan, her other hand fluttering over her tummy. Then she'd quieten again.

"Hold on, Sal. Four more days. That's all. You just need to hold on for four more days." I kissed the back of her hand and finally allowed the tears to fall.

THIRTY-THREE

An Envelope in the Church

I stayed with Sally for the rest of the morning, holding her hand while she fitfully slept. Wendy came back after a few hours, her eyes swollen and a tissue clutched in one hand. I relinquished my seat beside Sally and left the sisters to say their peace to each other.

Besides, I had places to go. I drove from the hospital to the church, ignoring the hunger pains in my stomach. Maybe the machine had recharged early. What if it had? I could admit the truth to Wendy and together we could get Sally here. Fix her, and not just from the overdose.

My key struggled in the lock as usual, and then the door swung open and the first thing I noticed was the envelope on the floor.

Thinking it was probably junk mail of some sort I picked it up. The envelope was A4 size, and creamy white, an expensive paper, not the sort you'd find a double glazing leaflet inside. There was nothing on the front, no name, not even: to the occupier. I ripped the flap open and pulled out a wad of papers, a second key falling out from the bottom.

"Oh my God," I muttered. Realizing the door was still wide open I closed it and on a whim used the new key to lock up. "Huh." I popped the key in my pocket and took the post over to my favorite seat. During the week I'd moved one of the pews so that I had the perfect view, with the pod in the foreground and the cross directly behind. If I squinted it seemed as if Jesus had his feet resting on the lid.

The first page was a title page and simply said: *To the current Key Holder*. Then underneath it said: *In the event of the death of Richard Newland*. How very odd. I flipped over and started reading through the following pages. There was a lot of legal jargon that I had to admit I didn't understand. But the gist, if I understood it, was that the pod was to be signed over to the current key holder – which was me.

There was a separate document that needed to be taken to a named solicitor. I'd sign and be witnessed, and the church and contents would become mine. And there was further provision to carry on this method of ownership in the event of my death. On top of that I would then be named as caretaker. I flipped the page to find that as caretaker, I would be paid.

"Seriously…?" I scanned the document again. No, I'd read right the first time. My wage would be more than I'd ever earned in my previous life as a teaching assistant.

And, to go along with owning the church and becoming the caretaker, there was a generous fund for repairs. The church was to be kept looking neglected, but in a safe state. The papers explained this was to keep the church from being noticed. The fund had so many zeroes behind the initial number that I had to look twice. All repairs had to go through the named solicitor, and seemed very secure. No sneaking money out of this fund.

"Bloody hell." I put the papers down and stared up at Christ. "This is huge," I said. "I'm not sure I'm the right one for the job. Look what's happened since I've had the key."

This was more responsibility than I think I'd ever had in my life. I thought of Janie, she'd be far more suited to this than me. She was caring and compassionate and reliable. She thought of others and set about making a difference. With me having Jimmy around, who knows what would happen in the future? What if he got another urge to poke around in the machinery? Since I knew him he'd been talking about how one way or another he'd make millions. Over the years he'd tried to perfect various inventions and ideas. If he had this wonderful pod within his reach how long before he tried to copy it? He didn't have the expertise to go it alone, so it would be him and Bob in league against me. I wouldn't stand a chance.

"What do I do?" My words echoed around the church.

Christ didn't seem to be in an answering mood today. He hung there from his cross, his expression pained, yet there was peace there, a serene expression hidden in the torture that I'd not noticed before.

"Okay, I'll do it. But make a deal with me. Help me. Can you do that? Make sure I don't cock this up."

That Elusive Cure

Silence filled the church, and as I stared up at the cross the sun broke through the clouds and streamed through the stained glass windows, blanketing Christ in a rainbow of colors.

"That'll do for me. Thank you," I said. Dipping my head in respect I took a moment of reflection before gathering the papers and leaving.

THIRTY-FOUR

Sally's Getting Worse

I slept badly. Wendy called late Friday and brought me up to date. Sally's liver function was beginning to deteriorate. Her kidney function was worsening as well. This could well be the start of multiple organ failure, and not a good sign.

The pod came to me in my dreams, taunting me with its super powers and mending an ever-lengthening stream of patients. A queue had formed, one that seemed to go on forever, stretching out the church, around Birkenhead and beyond. When I tried to get Sally to the pod, I was met with polite smiles then told to get to the back of the queue. Someone was selling trinkets in the car park. They had miniature pods on sale and fridge magnets with the words: I've been to the pod and survived. There were t-shirts and pictures of the church. The stall owner grinned widely at me, displaying gaps where he was missing teeth. The waiting people reminded me of people I'd seen in pictures as they waited at Lourdes and other holy places. The cripples and the infirm, the diseased and the insane, all hoping for a miracle.

I woke up in a sweat, knowing exactly why the pod had to remain a secret. There were only three days to go until Sally could be cured. I had to hope that her damaged body survived until then.

Knowing that I wouldn't have the result I so desperately wanted, I went to the church anyway. The sun was still only just peeking above the horizon. I'd left Jimmy asleep in bed, and here I was hoping for the impossible.

The hatch slid open and closed as smoothly as ever. Then the female voice, so familiar that she also visited me in my dreams, spoke.

"Power restarting. Diagnostics initiating. Pressure in the nanoparticle chamber is 99% and functionality is restored. Nanoparticle density is 90% and not high enough for functionality. Estimated time to recharge nanoparticles is three days. Recommend recharging with MicroHealth nanoparticles. Please contact MicroHealth representative."

"No!" I yelled. "That's not right, you need to be done. I need you to work!"

Rage boiled inside of me, so hot it burnt my cheeks and seemed to almost blind me.

I ran at the pod, the urge to rip and tear irresistible. At the last moment, some part of me saw sense and I veered away from the pod and ran at the stack of pews to my left instead. I tore at the benches. One near the top came loose and fell my way. It thudded into me and unable to keep my footing, the bench and I collapsed as one, my head bouncing off the floor as I hit. The pew knocked the wind out of me as it crashed on top of me.

I'm not sure how long I lay on the floor. When I opened my eyes grey snow filled my vision. The back of my head throbbed – that's what woke me up. I felt carefully and found a tender swollen lump.

"It's not fair, she's dying and I can't do anything about it." Tears filled my eyes. "All I want to do is save her. That's it. Just Sally. I'd give up my last session for her. I would have given up all my sessions for her."

The bench was stopping me from breathing properly. I pushed at it, but there seemed to be no strength in my arms and the pew hardly moved. So this was how it was going to end. With me trapped in a church, the only keys in my handbag and a pod right next to me that would have saved me in a couple of days, should I manage to crawl out from under the bench.

Jesus stared down at me, his face passive.

"I'm not sure I can go on without Sally. It'll be my fault if she doesn't make it." Tears flowed freely. "I can't cope, being this close to the magic and unable to use it."

The bone-white paint that had been used on His tunic was peeling. The blood dripping from His head had faded to a deep brown. If I got out from under this pew I'd get Him restored. I had to leave the outside of the building unimpressive. That didn't mean I couldn't put the inside back to the way it should be.

I tried to push the pew off my chest again. Somehow I found the strength and shoved it far enough to the side for me to slide out from underneath. Guess my end was not going to be today.

That Elusive Cure

After one last check of the back of my head for blood and a quick test to make sure I wasn't concussed, I locked up and left for the hospital.

Sally's skin had begun to turn jaundiced, like a new-born baby. Between the air mattress and the drips, now up to two like the elderly lady in the end bed, and the weight she'd lost since I'd seen her at her house, she appeared like a small child. How long ago was it that we ate cake and laughed? Couldn't be that long ago. I held her hand, trying not to wake her, and settled into the visitor's chair.

I wondered when Wendy would show up. Maybe she'd bring the kids. My heart hurt when I thought about them. Poor kids. First their dad, and now their mother. They were going to be damaged forever.

The doctor had told Wendy that if she made it five days the chances started to be in her favor again. Today must be the third day, only two to go. I pictured Jesus in my church, concentrated on Him and asked Him to please give Sally a chance. She deserved it. She should get put in the pod, she needed to get better.

I must have squeezed her hand too hard while concentrating and I woke to find her head turned to the side, her blue eyes gazing at me.

"Making deals for my life?"

How did she know? She always did have a knack of reading my thoughts.

No point hiding the facts. "Yup. Asked God to give you a chance."

"And what did your god say?"

I shrugged. "Well nothing, not yet. We'll see if you get past day five. Then we'll have the answer."

She chuckled quietly. "Good luck with that."
Sally closed her eyes again, dozing while I sat next to her, watching the sun rise in the sky.

THIRTY-FIVE

Making a Wish

"Kath, it's Wendy."

I'd been out in the garden, watering flowers and deadheading when the phone rang.

"What's wrong?" Did I really need to ask? Did I want to ask? The answer was *no* both times, and yet I asked anyway.

"Sally isn't well. You should probably come to the hospital."

"I'm coming." Tossing my gardening gloves on the kitchen counter, I shouted into the living room where Jimmy was watching the football. "I've got to go to the hospital."

He appeared in the doorway as I changed my shoes. "Need me to come?"

I thought about it for a moment as I laced my trainers. "No, don't come. If it's what I think then the room will be full enough. I imagine Wendy's got the kids there."

Jesus, this sucked. Poor Peter and Lucy. I imagined them by the bedside trying to make sense of the shell that had been left behind. And their mother, once such a vibrant woman, now relying on machines to keep her alive. Everything about this was wrong.

I got onto the ward easily. Seems if a patient was close enough to death then visiting hour rules no longer applied. I'd given up wondering if the pod would have fixed her. With two days to go before the damn machine finished producing stupid nanoparticles, and Sally having apparently run out of time, the entire matter was moot. The whole situation fucking sucked.

Wendy had Lucy in her arms and Peter stood next to her. As I arrived, Lucy squirmed out of her aunt's arms and onto the bed. She snuggled up against her mother and was rewarded by a faint smile behind an oxygen mask.

Wendy looked up as I entered the room. She moved Peter to the other side of the bed. "Why don't you hold your mum's hand while I talk to Auntie Kathy, okay?"

With the two kids flanking their mother, Wendy took me to a day room.

"It's not looking good," she said. Wendy looked so tired, I wondered if she'd slept. "I remember the day Dad passed. Did Sally tell you how he died?"

I did remember, in far too much detail. But I knew what Wendy needed and shook my head.

"I found him. He'd done it behind his shed. I was sixteen years old and had come home from a date with this boy called Ronnie. He was my first love. Ronnie from Greasby. He was tall and dark and handsome and he treated me like a princess." She stared wistfully over my shoulder. "Ronnie had kissed me for the first time and I wanted to tell Dad. Dad and I were close, really close to the point where Mum was jealous of our relationship. Mum was in the house looking after Sally. She was just a baby at the time, not even a year old. I went out to the garden and couldn't find him in the shed. Then I heard this strange bumping-banging sound coming from behind the shed."

She stopped speaking and pressed a damp tissue against her eyes.

"He'd hanged himself from the apple tree. It was a windy night and the noise was his feet bumping against the shed. Mum had the apple tree cut down a few months afterwards. I cried more after she cut that tree down than after I found Dad. I think the tree had started to represent Dad. I'd go there after school and sit down beside the spot where he'd died and talk to him."

I took Wendy's hands, squeezing them gently. Sal had told me their dad had hanged himself, but I'm not sure even she'd known that Wendy found him. All these years Sal had been angry at Wendy and her mothering when really it seemed what she was doing was trying to protect her little sister.

"What's going to happen to those children?" Wendy asked me. "She wants you to have them, you know."

I did know. There was a will detailing the arrangements and what little money Sal had was to be used to raise them. When Cass was little she'd been named as guardian. When Peter and then Lucy were born, I'd been named as theirs.

"I don't want to lose them. They're all the family I've got."

"You think they should live with you instead?"

"I think that we should honor her wishes." She patted my hands.

"Wendy, I realize there was something going on between you and Sal that I don't really understand. But I've seen you with the kids. There is nothing wrong with your mothering instincts."

"You're kind, Kath. You know what you're doing and you're young. I'm nearly sixty. Looking after the children has near enough killed me these past few weeks. What I brought you in here to say was that she wants to make sure you'll have the children. Don't argue with her. These are her last moments. I want them to be as happy as possible, if not for her, then for the children. They will never forget these moments, not for the rest of their lives."

I nodded.

"Let's go back in," Wendy said.

We walked back in to the room, hand in hand. Lucy was still snuggled up against her mother. Peter was standing by the window, staring out at the park. Dog walkers were out, and a group of four dogs were bounding around on the grass while the owners stood on the path nearby.

"Hi Sally," I said, going around to the far side of the bed.

I tried to smile at Lucy, but it was so hard. The little girl squeezed her eyes closed and refused to acknowledge me.

Stroking Sal's hair, I tried to arrange it so it looked nice. Who wants to die with bed head? I glanced up to see Lucy had found a hair brush. She handed it over to me and I carefully tidied and smoothed her mother's dark hair under the little girl's watchful eye.

The day started to draw to a close. Sometime after lunch I'd sat in a chair on one side of the bed. Wendy was in another chair on the opposite side. Peter had curled up and gone to sleep on the still empty third bed. Lucy lay next to her mother, silent tears wetting her cheeks.

I thought Sally was asleep, and was surprised when her hand touched my arm. She pulled the mask off her face and smiled at me. "You'll have the kids when I'm gone."

"Of course I will. We agreed." I stroked her hair finding it hard to look her in the eye.

"They should call you Mummy Kath. None of this auntie business. They need a mother."

I nodded. "Yes, I'll make sure they do."

"Thank you." Her voice was weak. "I don't plan on dying tonight. You should all go home and get some rest."

Sal fell back into a coma-like sleep. Despite her telling us to go, we stayed until the summer sun gave way to a purple-blue twilight. A star appeared and I picked up Lucy and went to the window.

"See that? You can make a wish on the first star that appears each night, did you know that?"

Lucy shook her head.

"If you see it before the other stars appear you have to say a poem to get the wish. Would you like me to teach you so you can make a wish?"

Lucy nodded and stuck a thumb in her mouth.

"Okay, here goes. *Star light, star bright, first star I see tonight, I wish I may, I wish I might, have the wish I wish tonight.*"

Together we stared at the star.

"Did you make a wish, Lucy?"

The little girl nodded.

"I did as well. Let's hope our wishes come true."

In unison we looked back at Sally. Two more days. I just needed her to survive two more days.

THIRTY-SIX

A Belligerent Scientist

I went to the machine early Monday. With my mobile in my pocket I both wanted and didn't want a call from Wendy. My sleep that night had been fitful. I kept dreaming of Sally lying in her hospital bed, the pain uncontrolled. The doctor spoke with Wendy and me before we left Sunday night. He was surprised she'd pulled through as many days as she had. If she got through today the chances of her surviving the overdose began to rise.

That was why I was here, in the church, at six o'clock in the morning. For a while I didn't touch the pod. I didn't want it to say what I knew it would. That it wasn't fixed and wouldn't be until tomorrow. More than ever, Sally needed the damn pod to be working.

I'd made a deal with God and Jesus. I'd asked them to keep Sally going, and they seemed to be keeping up with their side of the deal. I sat on the pew, miraculous machine and religious symbol filling my sight. If I ignored the dust and piles of pews, the neglect and the lack of love the church had suffered from for goodness knows how long, I could see the way the church interior would be after I was done repairing it. No more peeling paint on Jesus. The red velvet replaced where you kneeled. The altar refurbished. To be honest I couldn't remember ever being in a church other than for births, deaths and marriages so wasn't entirely sure what needed to be done, or even what was missing.

Finally I got up and went to the back of the machine. I opened the hatch, waited a few seconds and then closed it.

The machine spoke, the voice seeming louder than ever in the quiet church. "Power restarting. Diagnostics initiating. Pressure in the nanoparticle chamber is 99% and functionality is restored. Nanoparticle density is 97% and not high enough for functionality. Estimated time to recharge nanoparticles is one day. Recommend recharging with MicroHealth nanoparticles. Please contact MicroHealth representative."

"No. You're wrong."

I opened and closed the hatch again.

The machine repeated its diagnosis. Still one day to go.

I opened and closed the hatch a third time.

The voice told me the same information. 97% full of nanoparticles. One day to recharge. Stupid machine.

I opened and slammed the hatch closed.

The words repeated.

"No! Tell me something different!" I shouted and opened and slammed the hatch closed.

The same words. I had them memorized. I could say them along with the woman.

That Elusive Cure

"Be fixed!" I yelled and opened and slammed the hatch again.

On some level, I knew I was being as stupid as Jimmy when he'd had a yank at the pipe inside the machine. I was going to break something and then I'd be back to who knows how long until the stupid functionality was restored. I backed off, coming to rest against an askew pew. Tears didn't flood down my cheeks, even though I felt like they should be. Sally was in the hospital and her life seemed to be hanging from the proverbial thread. I could almost picture it, a golden thread wrapped around her heart and connecting her to the heavens. When would it snap? Today? Tomorrow? Or would that golden thread somehow give her years?

I pulled my phone from my pocket and rang the ward. As ever the phone at the other end took ages before someone picked up.

"Hello, I was wondering if someone could give me some information about Sally Jones."

"Yes, I can help. Who are you?"

"I'm Kathy Wyatt... um... one of her sisters," I said remembering what Wendy had told me. "How is she today?"

"Just a minute, let me find her chart."

I hung on while the nurse searched for the information. The shifts changed around this time, so I guessed she was fresh on for the day shift.

"Sally is still critical, but no worse through the night."

"Does that mean she's beating this?" Without thinking I crossed my fingers.

"It's too soon to say that, sorry."

"Okay. Thanks." I hung up and sat on the floor a while longer, until my bottom went numb and my stomach let out a rumble that reminded me that I needed to eat. Nine o'clock had come and gone. Jimmy would be up by now, working in his study and wondering where I was.

I made my way home, and found Jimmy in the kitchen making scrambled eggs for breakfast.

"I had a thought while you were gone," he said as I walked in. "Maybe Newland had machines set up all over the country, and all of them are now being looked after by the current user, just like you? It would explain how you hear about spontaneous remissions. Maybe they're all using pods?"

"Seriously? With everything going on right now, that's what you think about?" I accepted the cup of tea he gave me and sat at the kitchen table.

He shrugged.

"I hadn't thought of that, but kind of makes sense, I suppose."

The phone rang and I froze. Bad news, good news? I picked up and with Jimmy keeping an unwavering eye on me said, "Hello?"

"It's me, Bob. Look I have a bit of an emergency. I need some more of those nanoparticles today. I can be there just after lunch and you can take me to the pod. Do all your cloak and dagger stuff and blindfold me if it makes you feel any better."

"Bob?" I'd all but forgotten about him. "Sorry Bob, but you can't have any more particles."

"It recharges, of course I can. I need them for my research. I made a breakthrough last night, but need a fresh supply. The vial Jimmy gave me wasn't very pure. I think that's where I've been having problems. I can draw a concentrated sample using lab equipment. Don't worry, the machine won't be harmed."

"Now's not the time, Bob. Call back in a week."

"I don't have a week. You don't understand, I'm on the cusp of figuring out the beauty. I need more to work with."

"No, Bob. You're not understanding me. *Not right now.*"

"Kath, this is ground-breaking stuff going on here. I'd explain but you wouldn't understand-"

I interrupted. "No, Bob. You're the one that doesn't understand. Look forget it. If you can't wait a week then that's it. Forget it." I hung up and sagged back against the chair. "What a git. Did you hear that? Couldn't wait a week to get a new sample of particles."

The phone rang again. Jimmy made a move to answer it, but I got there first. I was in no mood for a belligerent scientist. "What?"

"If you don't let me get a sample I'm going to the press."

I sat up. "Why would you do that? If you take it to the press you'll ruin it for everyone."

"This invention deserves to be out there and available for everyone."

"Don't you understand, if it became public you'd never get close to the machine again. It'd either be swallowed up by some government organization we've never heard of, or it would be swamped with the sick."

"Just let me get my sample and we don't have to worry about either of those scenarios."

"Are you really that much of an asshole? Really? This is your solution?"

I was about to hang up again when Jimmy caught my arm and snatched the phone from me. He put the handset on speaker and said, "Look if you went to the press there's a good chance they'd label you as a loony and you'd never be taken seriously as a scientist again."

"I'll tell them about the church."

"Okay. Where is the church?"

There was silence from the other end for a moment. "I'll tell them about you two."

"And what are we going to tell them?" I said.

"What church?" Jimmy smirked at me. "I don't know anything about a church."

There was another pause. Then Bob said, "Fine. I'll wait a week and then I'm phoning back, and you'd better give me access then."

Bob hung up.

Jimmy put the handset back in the cradle. "Don't look so concerned. Bob's not going to do anything. He doesn't want to lose the machine any more than we do."

I nodded, but privately I wasn't so sure.

THIRTY-SEVEN

Barred

Before the sun had properly come up I was at the church. I didn't bother with the hatch this time. Instead I triggered the lid, slipped off my shoes and climbed in. I'd forgotten how comforting the foam was as it expanded to hold me. I raised my left hand and placed my palm on the panel in the lid.

The pod sealed me inside and the machine said, "Patient recognized. Scan initiating."

I felt hollow. It should be Sally in here. Not me.

"Diagnosing."

This used to excite me. Like unwrapping a Christmas present, one that you were pretty sure of, but wouldn't know for certain what it was until the paper came off.

"Two tumors found in the liver of 19mm and 10mm."

At least they hadn't grown since the last scan.

"Session four of the five recommended. One remaining to fix cancer sites. One to reverse the stoma."

I sighed. How many sessions would Sal need? How many to make her whole again?

"Begin session?" the machine asked.

"Yes," I said.

Vibrations moved along my body. Now I had a clue as to how the machine worked, I imagined the air in the pod being pumped with nanoparticles. Saw them entering my body with each breath. Maybe they settled on the skin and wormed their way into my capillaries? The area around my liver went warm as the vibrations concentrated on that area. Sally's liver was failing. She was the one that needed this. Not me.

The machine stopped. "Session complete. Final session in three days' time."

The lid opened and I lay there for a long time staring at the ceiling.

Somehow I had to get Sally here now I knew it worked again. The fact that my body was now clear of cancer, a prospect I had thought would never again apply to me, didn't make me jump around shrieking with joy. I didn't crumple and cry with relief. I didn't really experience any emotions, just an emptiness that made me sad.

I got to the hospital early and found Sally asleep. The third bed was filled now. A young woman lay there, and if I had to guess, she'd been the victim of a horrific road accident.

But Sally was my concern. Her skin had gone from merely jaundiced to an awful deep yellow color. Her breath crackled, and she struggled with each one. A clip on her finger was monitoring her pulse and oxygen levels. Even with the mask on, the percentage of oxygen in her system wasn't going above eighty-five percent, her pulse staying above one hundred. The worst part was the smell. There was a scent about her that was musky. It filled the room, emanated from her skin and tainted her breath. The odor of an approaching death.

Time was running out.

A nurse came in, and I called her over. "Would it be possible for me to put Sally in a wheelchair and take her outside for some fresh air?"

"Sorry, but your sister is far too poorly for that." She turned around and attended to the new arrival.

I'd seen so many movies where patients were freed from hospitals. It seemed so easy. Put some day clothes on them, help the patient limp out. Put them in a wheelchair and simply push them out. Get a friend to help and force their way out.

"Hey Sally." I stroked her arm, trying to wake her up.

She groaned and her eyes flickered open.

"I can make you better. You just need to trust me. Can you stand?"

Sally gave me a weak sarcastic look and without saying a word squeezed my hand. Her grip was so weak I almost missed it.

"Okay. Then I'm going to get a wheelchair. Be right back."

I went to the corridor and spied a chair. Checking that the nurses were otherwise occupied, I took it back to the room.

Over the last couple of days Sally had acquired more tubes. She now had a catheter and as I lifted the bed covers, I realized she was wearing an adult nappy. A faint smell of poo met my nose. She had a nutrients drip and a saline drip. There was a morphine pump that I assumed the nurses were administering, because I didn't think Sally had the strength for the button. All these wires and tubes. How was I going to get her in the chair?

As I tried to help her sit up I realized they'd hooked her up to a heart monitor. More wires emerged from under her hospital nighty and fed to pads stuck to various places on her chest.

"Come on. I'm going to need you to help. Do you want to live?"

Sally's mouthed the word, "*Yes*," from under her oxygen mask.

I unhooked the bag of urine and found a place to hang it on the wheelchair. I got the drips swapped over. Hoping some kind of alarm wouldn't blare out, I unplugged the heart monitor. I waited for a loud sound, but none came. It kept doing its thing. Must have a battery pack, I decided and unsure how I was going to push the wheelchair and the heart monitor at the same time started to help Sally into the chair.

"What do you think you're doing?" The nurse came in, put the tray of meds she was carrying on a counter and came at me. "Sally is very sick, you're going to kill her if you try and move her."

"But you don't understand, I need to get her out of here." I tried to wrestle her off Sally.

The nurse reached over and pressed a red button. Another nurse came running into the room.

"Call security. Now!"

"No, you don't understand, I can make her better." I grabbed at Sally. If I could get her in the chair, I could wheel her out, before security came.

That Elusive Cure

"Are you insane? She needs to be in a hospital." The nurse put herself in between me and Sally. Her strength surprised me. I couldn't get past her no matter what I tried.

Two men came in, their arrival far quicker than I had thought possible. They flanked me, each grabbing an arm and dragging me away from Sally.

"No, you can't do this! You'll kill her. I need to get her out of here. I've got a machine, I can mend her!" I screamed at the nurses as the security men dragged me away.

They took me to a small room where I had to give my details and was told if I stepped foot inside the hospital again I would be arrested. My picture was taken and I had to sign away my rights to use that hospital. With the paperwork finished, the security men escorted me out the main doors and watched as I made my way to my car.

"Bastards!" I shouted and kicked a curb. They were still keeping an eye on me. I flicked them a two finger salute, but the pair of them merely raised their eyebrows.

I sat in the car and decided I'd leave when I was good and ready. My phone rang and I checked the screen to see Wendy was on the line. Shit. The hospital must have phoned her. I could ignore her call. Turn off my phone and not go home. But if I could convince Wendy, take her to the machine, show her what it was capable of then maybe she'd help me get Sally there.

"Hello?"

"What the hell do you think you were up to? Do you realize you could have killed her?" Wendy screamed though the phone, I had to hold the handset away from my ear.

"Wendy, I have a plan. Let me come and get you. I've got to show you something. I've got a machine. I can fix Sally. Make her better, like none of this happened. You have to trust me."

"A machine? You've got a machine?" She let out a sharp laugh.

"Yes, I do. I'll come and get you and show you."

"Oh yes, sounds perfectly normal. Let me get my coat."

Thank God. If I could get Wendy on board, together we stood a chance of getting Sally there. "What a relief-"

"You think I'm serious? Kathy, you almost killed Sally today. All her vitals are worse. She was just beginning to beat this thing, and you've made everything worse."

"But Wendy, I've got a machine, I can fix her."

She laughed again. "You're as crazy as my sister."

"I'm not, this is real. Let me take you there."

"Understand me. I'm not going anywhere with you. You're not going to go anywhere near my sister. In fact stay away from all of us."

"No, Wendy…"

She ended the call.

"Shit." I hit the steering wheel. This was not the way this was supposed to go.

THIRTY-EIGHT

Sally

The phone rang at five fifty-three the next morning.

I answered, knowing whose voice would greet me.

"Kathy, I thought you should know. Sally has died. She stopped breathing about half an hour ago."

"Oh Wendy. I'm so sorry."

Wendy started sobbing. "She's at peace now."

Jimmy got out of bed and put his arms around me. I started to weep at his touch.

"She's with Dad now," Wendy said, her voice breaking.

Through the tears I thanked her for calling. I hung up and collapsed crying against Jimmy.

THIRTY-NINE

A New Future

Four months later:

"Come on, kids, time to go." I checked the clock, we were going to be late if they didn't hurry up.

I dashed upstairs and found Lucy on the footstep examining her teeth in the mirror.

"Are they clean, Mummy Kath?" she asked and leaned in, teeth bared. The mirror fogged up and hid her image. She turned to me and opened wide for me to check.

"They are perfect," I said and tossed her the hand towel to dry her face. "Come on, you're going to be late."

Peter was in his room, digging through the mess for an exercise book. "I can't find my maths book. I'm going to get a lunchtime detention if I don't have it."

I couldn't believe that in three short months, Peter had managed to create so much mess. "Come on, move over." Kneeling down I shoveled through the clothes and toys and pulled out a blue book. "Here it is!"

"Thanks." He shoved it in his school bag. "Can you find my English book now?"

Somehow I got them to school just as the bell went. Lucy gave me a long hug then ran off after her brother. Nerves fluttered in my tummy. Today was the day I would finally pass on the key. I put the car in gear and drove off towards the motorway.

Twenty minutes later I pulled into the car park outside the oncology building at Clatterbridge. For weeks I'd been thinking about who I wanted to give the key to. Janie said she'd picked me because I reminded her of her mother when she was young. Her finder picked her because she looked like his daughter. What was I looking for? A newly-retired person? A really sick person? A young person? A man? A woman? It was too much responsibility. Whoever I picked would be lucky and that meant I'd be allowing others to die or face the long battle without the help of the pod.

By the entrance there was the usual scattered group of smokers. One person sat in a wheelchair, hooked up to an IV, pulling her dressing gown around skinny legs with one hand whilst holding a cigarette with the other. A gaunt man sat on the bench puffing away. I certainly wasn't going to help one of them. They weren't even trying to beat this disease. I thought about going straight up to the Delamere Ward where I used to go, but decided what I really needed first was a cup of tea.

Sitting outside the café on the ground floor, I realized I was in the best place possible to patient-watch. Nursing my tea, I studied people as they came in the entrance and made their way to various destinations in the hospital. Most had a partner with them, a husband, wife, adult child or friend. It was easy to pick out the poorly one.

About half an hour after I'd sat down, and still no closer to making a decision, I watched as a young mum came into the hospital pushing a child of around Lucy's age in a wheelchair. It was hard to tell whether the child was a girl or boy, they were so thin, so pale, their skin the shade of an antique porcelain doll. The child wore a colorful scarf to cover their scalp, and a drip line snaked out from a sleeve and up to a bag of medicine hung from an elevated hook.

I thumbed the key, watching as the mother and child went towards one of the downstairs wards. This was it. My heart pounded, my breath grew short. The key now clenched in one hand, I got up and followed them down the hall.

FORTY

The Headlines

Two years later:

22nd Oct – Could nanoparticles be curing us in the next decade? Breakthrough in nanotechnology as scientists cure tumor-ridden mice.

Four years later:

10th October – English scientist Dr. Robert Handler is surprise winner of the Nobel Prize in Medicine for work in medicinal use nanotechnology.

Five years later:

3rd May – Nobel Prize winning scientist Dr. Robert Handler unveils prototype for a miraculous healing scanner. Using nanotechnology most illness can be cured with just a few painless sessions. Hailed the most important invention of all time. Handler is lauded.

12th September – Nobel Prize winner Dr. Robert Handler outed as a fraud. Miracle machine used to con investors out of millions proved to be a fake.

24th September – Shamed scientist Dr. Robert Handler stripped of his Nobel Prize.

30th September – Disgraced scientist Dr. Robert Handler found dead in his home after suspected suicide. The police aren't looking for anyone in connection with his death.

Six years later:

15th January – Eighty-nine year old Oscar winning actor Steve Williams in remission from terminal lung cancer despite chain smoking for over seventy years. Puts his miraculous recovery down to eating well and a positive attitude.

About the Author

Lisa C Hinsley's career has been varied, working as an architectural technician, a pet sitter, a pharmacy supervisor and most recently a carer/companion for elderly ladies, all the while writing when she can. Born in Portsmouth in 1971, Lisa grew up in England, Scotland, and America. She now lives on the Wirral, in northwest England, with her husband, three children, four cats and a dog.

You can find out more about Lisa C Hinsley here:

Website:
www.lisahinsley.weebly.com
Facebook:
https://www.facebook.com/LisaHinsley.author
Twitter:
@LisaCHinsley

If you enjoyed *That Elusive Cure*, please let Lisa know at lisa@hinsley.org and leave a review on the book's page.

Printed in Great Britain
by Amazon.co.uk, Ltd.,
Marston Gate.